THE
HUMPBACKED
FLUTEPLAYER

The Humpbacked Fluteplayer

SHARMAN APT RUSSELL

Alfred A. Knopf   New York

This is a Borzoi Book published by Alfred A. Knopf, Inc.

Copyright © 1994 by Sharman Apt Russell
Jacket illustration copyright © 1994 by Peter Catalanotto
All rights reserved under International and Pan-American
Copyright Conventions. Published in the United States by
Random House, Inc., New York, and simultaneously in
Canada by Random House of Canada Limited, Toronto.
Distributed by Random House, Inc., New York.

Map and decoration by Becky Terhune

Manufactured in the United States of America
10 9 8 7 6 5 4 3 2 1

Library of Congress Cataloging-in-Publication Data
Russell, Sharman Apt.
The humpbacked fluteplayer / Sharman Apt Russell.
p. cm.
Summary: While on a school field trip, May and Evan find
themselves transported to an alternative reality and are made
slaves by one of the warring Indian tribes who live
in the Arizona desert.
ISBN 0-679-82408-1 (trade)
1. Indians of North America—Arizona—Juvenile fiction.
[1. Indians of North America—Arizona—Fiction. 2. Space
and time—Fiction.] I. Title. PZ7.R91594Hu
1994 [Fic]—dc20 92-44492

For my daughter MARIA

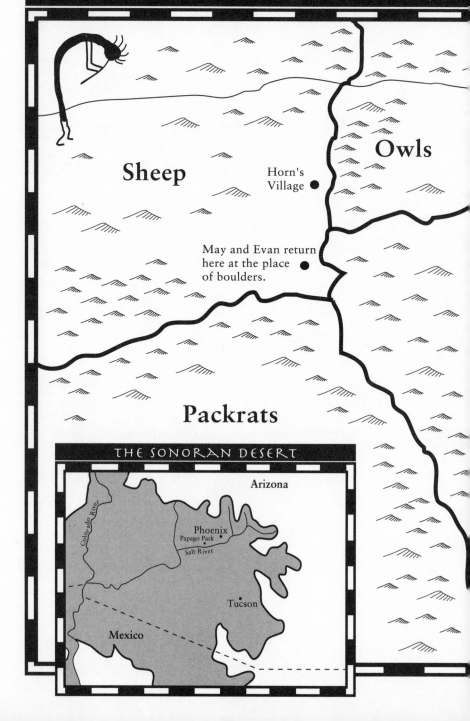

Sheep

Owls

Horn's
Village ●

May and Evan return
here at the place ●
of boulders.

Packrats

THE SONORAN DESERT

Arizona

Colorado River

Phoenix
Papago Park ●
● Salt River

Tucson ●

Mexico

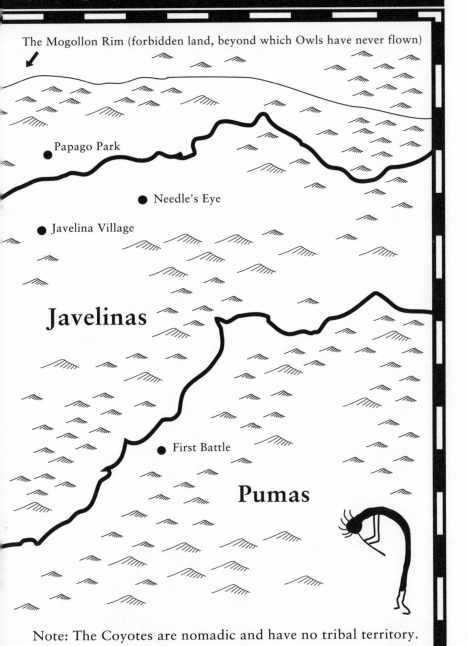

THE SIX TRIBES

The Mogollon Rim (forbidden land, beyond which Owls have never flown)

● Papago Park

● Needle's Eye

● Javelina Village

Javelinas

● First Battle

Pumas

Note: The Coyotes are nomadic and have no tribal territory.

PART ONE

LAND
OF THE
PAINFUL
MOON

ONE

May looked out over Papago Park, a chunk of desert set aside and preserved in the sprawling city of Phoenix, Arizona. From her seat on the concrete picnic bench she could see the buildings of the Phoenix Zoo that bordered the park about a mile away. She could hear cars swishing back and forth like trapped animals on the nearby highway. Between her and that highway stretched the desert, alive with mice, rats, snakes, scorpions, tarantulas, and a million thorny plants. Fat barrel cactus were covered with spines in the shape of fishhooks. Oval pads of prickly pear, low to the ground, bristled with sharp needles. An especially ugly plant that was as tall as May rose up in a tangle of twisted limbs: these, too, had thorns instead of leaves.

Papago Park! May thought angrily. They've got a lot of nerve calling this gravel pit a park!

In Philadelphia, where she had lived until last

December, parks were green. They had soft green grass and pretty flowers. In Philadelphia a spring breeze would be cooling her cheek. Here, on the first of May—the month she was named for—the sun beat down on a desert that was already as dry and brown as burned toast.

"Where I went to school before," May said to the blond girl sitting next to her on the picnic bench, "we took a really *good* field trip to the Morris Arboretum to see the daffodils."

The rustling of sandwiches, wrapped in wax paper, stopped for a moment.

"My parents had the director of the arboretum over for dinner," May went on. Again no one replied, not even their sixth-grade science teacher, who was busy with a thermos at the far end of the table. May opened her mouth, but a red-haired boy with glasses spoke first.

"What do your parents do now?"

The sandwiches, slapped together by the school's kitchen staff, were stale cheese on wheat bread. May bit into one reluctantly. She didn't want to talk about now. She wanted to talk about then.

"Back home," she said, "I was secretary of my class."

The blond girl rolled her eyes and began a conversation that didn't include May. The boy with glasses smiled to himself.

Where I went to school before, May thought, we had decent lunches. And I had lots of friends!

After everyone had eaten, the teacher made them save their brown paper bags. Then she led the students out into the desert. May held her arms close to her sides. To brush even lightly against a cactus was to come away with part of it sticking into your flesh or clothing. Their teacher moved confidently through this obstacle course and stopped before a tall plant with a thick fluted trunk. Its arms were raised to the sky.

How ridiculous! May thought. It looks like a frightened telephone pole!

She wanted to whisper this to someone beside her. But no one was there.

"I'm sure you recognize the sa-*war*-o." Mrs. Garcia's voice rose above the squeals of a small child's birthday party nearby. "That's spelled s-a-g-u-a-r-o, for those of you who are new to Arizona." She looked at May and then at a girl in lime-green shorts, who stepped forward to read a report.

May's attention wandered. She still felt hungry and began to plan what she would have for dinner. With their new jobs, her parents were rarely home before eight on weekdays. On these nights May could eat whatever she pleased. She was thinking of ice cream and frozen French fries when she heard the sigh of whispers. They rustled through the group like leaves in a wind.

"Queen May," a voice said. "That's a good name for her."

"Queen May ate daffodils for dinner!"

"Queen May was secretary of her class!"

"All hail, Queen May!"

The last was louder than the rest, and a gust of amusement shook the students.

"Questions?" the teacher asked sharply.

The girl in lime-green shorts finished her report in the sudden quiet. But the whispers did not stop. They only grew softer and somehow more awful. Mouths opened and closed silently. Murmurs barely touched the air.

"Queen May, Queen May, Queen May . . ."

As usual, May had dressed too warmly for the Phoenix weather. Now she felt the weight of her pants and the sweat trickling under her long-sleeved shirt. She blinked her eyes and stared at her white sneakers. With a supreme effort she kept her mouth from turning down.

"Thank you, Alison." Mrs. Garcia studied the class.

May cocked her head in a show of fake intense interest.

"Next," the teacher said, "Evan will tell us about the medicinal uses of desert plants."

The red-haired boy stepped out of the group and stood closer to the saguaro trunk. Tall and skinny, the boy had a freckled face and glasses fastened with an elastic sports band around the back of his head. His manner was confident. Everyone liked him.

"Well," he began, not bothering with notes, "the creosote bush is the most useful plant. The branches can be heated and put on joints and sore feet. The Papagos used them in childbirth. They also boiled or chewed the leaves to make a paste for snakebites. The cholla"—he pronounced it "*choy*-uh" and pointed at one of the bristly trees with twisted limbs—"was sometimes used as a cold medicine. The red blossoms of the ocotillo were made into a calming tea." This last name was said with a lilt, "o-kuh-*tee*-yo!"

May tried to listen now, if only to keep from hearing anything else. Perhaps she succeeded in this, or perhaps the others grew tired of their joke. As Evan's report went on, soothing and dull, May knew with relief that she was not going to cry. When Evan finished, the science teacher smiled at him affectionately.

Teacher's pet, May thought.

"You have your lunch bag." Mrs. Garcia suddenly became solemn. "And you can use it to collect one thing you would like to talk about in class tomorrow. We have special permission from the park to do this. Don't abuse it!"

Some of the students began to move, but the teacher held them on the leash of her voice.

"You have half an hour. That's all. Don't destroy any living plant. Don't bring back any live animal. Don't harm anything. Be particularly polite, please, to rattlesnakes and scorpions!"

A girl giggled dutifully.

"And be sure to stay *always*"—the teacher

paused for emphasis—"within sight of the picnic table!"

She stepped back and set the children free. They scattered into small groups, weaving and chattering through the jumble of plants. May looked at the ground. No one invited her to be part of a group, and she made herself walk away before Mrs. Garcia noticed her. The important thing was to avoid looking at anyone's face. The important thing was to get away, quickly, in any direction.

Unwillingly, she found herself going uphill.

It was hot! Her sticky skin rubbed against her clothes. Her chest tightened with grief. She didn't bother looking for something to put into her paper bag. It took all her energy just to pick a path through the prickly pear and barrel cactus. Unhappily she pushed at the brown bangs against her forehead. Far away, directly overhead, a plane flew north. May wished she could do the same.

Halfway to the top of the hill she had to pause and straighten her back. Below, the class had fanned out in a circle of exploration. No one looked up. Furious, May turned and began to make her way around the hill. Soon she could no longer see the concrete table with its benches and nearby water fountain. She hesitated, remembering her teacher's last warning. Then the class whispers came back to her: Queen May, Queen May. Bitterly she went on.

As May climbed, the gravelly slope turned more and more to solid rock. She slithered sideways, the boulders rough and warm when she touched them. Ahead, a dark spot showed in the side of the hill. The opening grew as she walked toward it, until its edges formed a black hole big enough for a person to enter.

It's a cave! May realized, happy to have reached some goal. Once more she paused and listened. No one called her name. "I'll just go and touch one wall," she muttered. "One wall and then I'll turn back."

The cave was farther away than it looked, and by the time May reached it her chest burned and she struggled for breath. She felt uneasy. How long had she been gone? Surely more than half an hour? Quickly she squeezed into the opening. Inside, the hole was not much deeper than a large closet. Still, May felt a cave's true coolness—and that certain hush of expectation.

In the shadowy light she did not immediately see the figure on the far wall. Only slowly, in the way that images waver and form underwater, did the drawing facing her become clear.

It was a man. Sticklike. Hunchbacked. With a flute to his lips. The big hump rose above the shoulder as the body stood sideways and the face turned to stare, full front, at the cave's intruder. The smile on the fluteplayer's face was sly and mocking and delighted. The round head with its circular eyes and dangling earrings seemed to pop up from a neck that stretched out longer than it should. The arms and legs were also too long. The fingers danced elegantly over the flute.

May thought of being scared. But the fluteplayer's smile was too comical, his eyes too mischievous. He was, after all, only a . . . pictograph. She remembered the word now. He was a picture drawn, perhaps hundreds of years ago, on a rock wall.

That's strange, May thought. No one had mentioned a pictograph in Papago Park. Could this drawing be undiscovered? Hidden here, in the middle of Phoenix? May went closer to trace the lines of the fluteplayer's hump. Still breathing hard, she did not hear the crunch of steps behind her. Carefully she put a finger to the tip of the flute. Just then a hand grabbed her other wrist and a voice said, "Hey! I've got you, Queen May."

A terrific explosion seemed to rip the hill apart. At first the noise was a crash of cymbals and drums. Then beneath it swelled a softer, higher sound.

Clear and sweet, the flute piped.

Clear and sweet, a melody grew until it became the world.

TWO

Someone groaned.

I'm hurt! May thought. I'm groaning!

She opened her eyes. She was sitting against hard rock. A body lay nearby. From the red hair she recognized Evan, the boy with glasses who had given the report on desert plants.

"Wha ha tha?" He groaned again.

Slowly May got to her feet and stood very still before twisting her back and waist. They worked fine. "Are you okay?" she asked Evan.

Like some trained bear he rolled over to crouch on all fours. Finally he stood up. "I guess so," he said in a shaky voice. Together, in slow motion, they stepped out of the cave.

The hill looked exactly the same as before the explosion. Evan pushed past May and took the lead back to the picnic grounds. May had to run to keep up. Near the bottom, around the side of the hill, the boy stopped. Behind his glasses, his blue eyes looked anxious. "It must be the other way," he said.

"Don't be silly!" May stared at the desert. "This is the way I came."

In the end they circled the hill twice before admitting the truth. The picnic grounds, the water fountain, the class, the teacher—they were all gone.

"That explosion!" May panted.

"But there's no *sign* of an explosion, no nothing!" Evan stood where there had once been a trash can on a cement slab. He kicked at the ground, sending up a swirl of dust. By now he looked as hot as May, his face red behind the freckles.

"What time is it?" May wondered.

Evan straightened and pointed his skinny arm. "See those bushes over there? You sit in the shade and wait," he ordered. "I'm going to get help."

"Don't tell *me* what to do!" May flared. "*You* sit in the shade and wait! I'm going to walk to the highway and get a ride." She marched off in the direction she happened to be facing.

"Great, fine!" Evan yelled at her. "But you're going the wrong way! Keep on if you want to get lost forever!"

May thought about not stopping. Then with an exaggerated shrug she turned. Evan set off without a word. Again May followed. Once more she had to concentrate to avoid the cactus and bruising rocks.

There are plenty of explanations for this, May

thought. There's no use thinking the worst. But every time she caught up to Evan, his face seemed grimmer and redder than before. Surefooted, he zigzagged through a patch of prickly pear. May scowled fiercely at his retreating back.

Without warning, Evan swerved toward a hill steeper than any around. "Going up here," he muttered.

"Wait!" May protested. But he was already climbing, bent over so far that he appeared headless above his white T-shirt. May stopped and for balance put her hand square on a barrel cactus. She screamed and plucked the thorns from her hand while Evan continued to the top of the hill.

There he stood for a long time.

"What do you see?" May called. Evan ignored her. Finally May struggled up the slope after him. Another cactus brushed her shoe, bit through the fabric, and held fast. "You stupid jerk!" May yelled up at Evan, who remained silent.

"What do you see?" she demanded again after she had reached the top. Now, of course, standing beside him, she could see for herself. "What do you see?" she repeated, suddenly worried.

"Nothing." Evan's voice was flat.

May stared out at the vista of rolling desert hills.

"Nothing," he repeated. "I don't see anything."

"Of course you do! What do you mean?"

"I mean, I don't see the gas station where it should be, or the Taco Bell, or the shopping mall. I don't see the downtown buildings. *I don't see Phoenix.*"

May had to smile. "You must be looking in the wrong direction."

"See that mountain over there?" Evan jabbed out a finger. "That's Camelback Mountain. I see that mountain every day from my window at home. I have a friend who lives there. He's rich. All the people who live on Camelback Mountain are rich. Do you see any houses there now?"

After this long speech, Evan shut his mouth as though he would never open it again. May stared at the view. Waves of hills rippled to join a far-off mountain range. Distance gentled the edges of rock so that the desert looked strangely soft—like a bolt of cloth flung out in colors of green, pink, tan, and lavender. In all of this there was not a glint of chrome, not a sign of buildings, people, or cars, not even a ribbon of road or highway. In all of this there was only silence and the roll of land. A breeze stirred May's damp hair. For the first time in her life she looked out on emptiness.

"There's plenty of good explanations for this," she whispered.

Evan squatted and put his head between his hands.

"Evan," May said after a moment. "I'm thirsty." She hesitated and then touched his shoulder. "We need water."

"I know. Let me think!" he murmured. "I used

to play in a canal by the gas station. No, there probably aren't any more canals. But the water came from somewhere—I guess from the Salt River that runs near the park. It should still be . . . here . . . a few miles south."

"Then come on," May said, taking charge. Although she tried not to show it, she didn't feel unhappy. She felt . . . like an adventurer in a book. "Come on!" She pulled Evan to his feet.

Silently he led May to a wash where sand filled their shoes and dragged at their legs. As they trudged for hours past endless hills, still they saw or heard no one.

"Not even any litter!" Evan said.

May found it easier to keep up with him now. He walked slowly and had to be prodded to give directions. By the time they reached the river, the setting sun had tinted it red and gold. The sight seemed to amaze Evan.

"I've never seen it like this," he marveled. "It's so big!"

The shallow water coursed swiftly over gravel and stone. Grass grew at the bank, and it was dotted with flowers—pink phlox and purple verbena. May saw green cottonwood trees on the other side of the river, just a little farther down. With cupped hands she knelt and drank again and again. The air felt so fresh! The water tasted so clean!

"Look." She began to explore. "Here's a place to cross. We could step on these stones."

"My family must be wondering where I am." Evan sat listlessly on the bank. "My brother's giving a concert tonight. He plays the saxophone."

"Evan," May said, "let's go over to the other side. We have to find a place to spend the night, and there are some trees on that bank. Get up! We should stay together."

Without looking back, she started to jump to the first stone. It was Evan's turn to follow.

"Do you have any brothers or sisters?" Evan's voice came from behind.

"No," May muttered. She eyed the distance to the next rock.

"I have four. Two brothers and two sisters."

"Good."

"Well, I don't think you care," he said. "This is just fun for you. Like something in a book. A big adventure."

May leaped to a flat rock big enough to hold them both. "Of course I care! I'm just not falling to pieces, that's all."

"Who's falling to pieces!" Evan said in a surprised tone.

"You are!"

"That's a laugh!"

"I'm not laughing!"

On either side of them the water rushed by. With a last flicker of light the sun disappeared behind a hill.

"Who got us to the river?" Evan asked. "Who—"

His face froze. He teetered and jumped to stand beside May. "Something moved over by those trees."

"Where?" May stared.

"On the other side! Where you wanted to camp!"

Quiet now, they looked hard at the shadows under the cottonwoods. A mass of roots sprawled there like twisting snakes.

"Hey!" May yelled so loudly that Evan started and almost fell.

Slowly two brown men emerged from behind the green-leafed trees. With hands in the air and palms out they walked carefully toward May and Evan. At the water's edge they stopped.

Short and broad, the men had powerful chests, thick arms, and muscular legs. Their black hair hung free. Except for loincloths, they were naked. For a moment they stood still, peering through the darkening air. Then they dropped to their knees. From this position, facing May and Evan, they bent low and salaamed like two humble worshipers.

THREE

The men pressed their noses to the earth again and again. After three bows, the larger of the two rose, spread his arms, and began to speak.

May and Evan looked at each other in dismay.

"What's he saying?" May asked.

"I don't know," Evan whispered.

Although the men kept their distance, they continued to plead and coax. At least that's what it sounded like to May. "Come, come, please, we won't hurt you," they seemed to be saying. "We welcome you! We greet you!" With a tender smile the larger pointed to himself and then to his companion.

May turned to Evan. "Should we?" she asked. Then she screamed. "Another one!"

Now a third man stood at the very spot where May and Evan had started to cross the river. He too watched them. But unlike the other men, he did not smile or make worshipful gestures. He did not even look friendly. His large head was capped by short brown hair, his nose was beaked, his yellow eyes were round and set widely apart. Feathers dangled from holes in his ears, and a cloth tunic covered his body from neck to knees. From the riverbank he stared at May and Evan with obvious distaste.

On the opposite side the two men jumped up in alarm and retreated slightly to the clump of cottonwoods. As they retreated, they shook their fists and howled.

The newcomer shot them a look of contempt. He spoke a word, and the men fell silent.

The round eyes under the brown hair blinked slowly at May and Evan. This man did not speak English either. But again May thought she could sense the meaning of his words. "Hurry," he seemed to urge without warmth. "Hurry! You are wasting my time!" His arm motioned to his side of the river.

"He wants us to go with him," Evan said.

"I can see that!" May answered. "Why doesn't he just come and get us? Why is everyone waiting for us to decide?"

On the flat rock in the middle of the water, they drew closer together.

"We seem to have a choice." Evan thought for a second. "Maybe the stream is some kind of neutral ground? A border they can't cross?"

That was a clever idea, and May nodded. "But which should we choose?" she asked doubtfully.

The man with the feathered earrings watched them, his face expressionless. The worshipers dropped to the ground. Their voices seemed to call out to May in soft tones. They seemed to be pleading, begging, asking her to come, come, for she was their queen long awaited.

"Evan! Let's go with these guys. At least they seem to want us."

Evan hesitated.

"Don't you see? They think we're gods or royalty or something. Like the Aztecs thought Coronado was a god."

"Cortés," Evan corrected. He looked back and forth from the indifferent single man to the two figures bowing and beckoning. The river ran past them, its shallow blue pools turning to black. May's face was sunburned, and her legs ached from climbing the desert hills. She was also very hungry.

"Come, come," the men on the ground seemed to coax.

"Let me think!" Evan fretted.

"There's no time!" May declared. "I'll go! I'll decide if you won't."

She jumped to the nearest rock, slipping a little in her haste. Clumsily she jumped to the next stone, the next, and the next.

"We should stay together," Evan called, and started after her. By the time she reached the shore, he was splashing behind.

Before leaving the river, May turned to look back.

In that second she saw the strange brown-haired man lift his arms and disappear. In his place an owl fluttered its wide wings. It hooted loudly and flew straight up into the sky.

May screamed again and fell against Evan. This isn't an ordinary field trip! she thought wildly. This isn't Phoenix!

Evan caught May in surprise and then rudely let her fall. "Ahem," he said as though he were about to make a speech to the two men hurrying toward them.

"Didn't you see that?" May shouted. "That man turned into an owl!"

"Shhh!" Evan gestured at her to be quiet even as a muscular arm reached out and grabbed him by the neck.

The next thing May knew, another arm had grabbed her as well and she was being picked up and carried back to the cottonwood trees. For a moment she caught a glimpse of Evan—dangling like a bag over his captor's shoulder.

At the trees the men got out coils of rope, which they used to tie her and Evan's ankles and wrists. They also retrieved long spears, which they had hidden in the tangle of roots. These spears were dagger-sharp, as one man demonstrated by pressing a point to May's leg. When she whimpered, he laughed.

Then he lifted her up again, holding her feet in an iron grip. Her head bounced hard against his back.

The darkness settled in quickly now. The trees blurred to rock and the rock to sky. Single file, the men set off at a jog.

FOUR

Even in her shock May was alert enough to wonder how the men could find their way so easily through the starlit night. Once she craned her neck and could just make out the faint outline of a trail leading deeper into the desert, away from the river. As the hours passed, her thoughts became less and less clear. Her head ached. Her wrists and ankles chafed against the rope. Every part of her body felt bruised and sore from the jolting trip.

At long last the men slowed to a walk. With a sudden jerk of her captor's shoulder, May fell to the ground in front of a small campfire. Evan fell beside her.

The two men lifted their spears and yelled. In the fire's glow May saw the round curves of huts and brush houses. She heard bare feet padding on hard-packed ground swept clear of cactus. Soon a ring of bodies surrounded her. Like the men, the women had brown skin, flat noses, and glittering dark eyes. Their black hair ribboned bare breasts. Their eyebrows were thick black lines. The older children stared and giggled. The small babies cried and clung to their mothers' hips. It was late, and the village seemed half asleep.

Evan's captor played with his spear. Lightly he jabbed it at May while his companion made a speech to a fat-faced man wearing a heavy copper necklace. May tried to press herself into the earth. She dreaded the touch of that sharp blade. The dirt beneath her hands ground against her scraped skin. The thought of being speared sickened her. Where would it go? Into her stomach? Into her chest? Into her leg?

Above her the ring of faces smiled approval. From May's view on the ground, these short, stocky people towered like giants, monstrous in the firelight. When they opened their mouths to laugh, their teeth looked huge. One woman had a scar that puckered her entire cheek. She came closer than the rest and studied May like a housewife inspecting a piece of meat at market.

When the two spearmen stopped their boasting, the man in the necklace knelt beside Evan to look at his blue and white shoes. Carefully he touched the dirty canvas. Then he boldly grabbed hold and pulled the sneakers off. Evan's eyes squeezed shut. May felt someone pull the shoes and socks off her own feet. Satisfied, the leader nodded, and the scarfaced woman undid May's ropes and helped her up.

Evan was also standing now, his glasses dangling from the sturdy band around his neck.

Suddenly the crowd seemed to lose interest. The villagers melted back into their huts, and the chief yawned as he muttered something to the men with spears. Grinning, the scar-faced woman pushed May away from the fire. One man carried a torch that lit the ground, while a second man followed behind.

Confused and barefoot, May rubbed her sore wrists. A sharp point pricked her back, and she whirled, crying out, "Leave me alone! Stop it!" Another point must have pricked Evan, for he pulled her forward.

The woman laughed and walked on ahead, leading them to a tall fence wavy and distorted in the torchlight. Before the fence stood a boulder as big as a school desk. The two men put down their spears to push the stone away, and May heard the noise of a gate swinging open. She felt a weight against her shoulder—and was shoved into darkness.

Briefly the torchlight lit the enclosure. Then the light vanished. In a panic May turned to pound on the closed gate.

"Don't touch it!" Evan warned as May found her fist impaled on thorns. She whimpered. "Pull loose," Evan ordered. "It's a fence made of ocotillo branches. My granddad has one. Pull! There's nothing else you can do."

With a gasp May pulled, leaving blood and skin on the thick thorns of the ocotillo fence. Sucking her fist, she stood as still as possible. There was no moonlight tonight. Only the stars shone high above. May strained to see in the darkness, blacker now after the torch's flare. Her heart thudded so hard that she could feel it beating in the small wounds of her hand. In the distance an owl hooted. May shuddered. That owl-man by the river with his round yellow eyes! His wings had stretched as wide as she was tall!

"Evan," she whispered. "I saw that man disappear. I saw—"

"Look!" Evan interrupted.

"What?" May wanted to escape so badly that she had to fight the impulse to pound again on the thorny gate. Just then three darker, blacker shapes emerged from the darkness: three figures also imprisoned by the ocotillo thorns. Slowly, as May cradled her hand, the forms of these other children became clear.

One was a girl as tall as May, with thin arms and legs and a skirt that hung loosely.

Behind her stood a figure who was nearly man-size, his shoulders broad and his arms thick.

In front of these two a little boy pranced forward. His hair caught bits of starlight and his teeth were bared in a foxy smile.

"Hello?" Evan tried.

"Hello!" May was more aggressive.

The bigger boy gave a grunt and dropped to the

ground. The girl chattered in the same language as the spearmen.

"Oh, speak English!" May snapped. "English! English!"

Abruptly the girl fell silent.

"Forget it," Evan said. "If they're here, then they're like us. Kidnapped. Prisoners."

"But we have to talk to them!" May said nervously. "To find out who they are! To find out where we are!"

"I don't care," Evan murmured, and May felt his body slide past hers. "I'm going to sleep."

"Sleep?" May couldn't believe him. "But what about these kids? What about that man? I saw him fly!"

Evan made no answer, at least not to her. His voice came muffled as though his head were sheltered deep in his arms. "Maybe if I go to sleep," he said, "I'll wake up and this will all be gone. This is a dream. I'll be home in my own room."

May thought that he might be crying. She crouched down beside him. Her hand burned. The owl hooted again. The other children in the enclosure were silent.

Exhausted, May curled up beside Evan. For a long time she lay there, her eyes wide open.

Then, when she thought about it next, it seemed that the darkness had grown even darker. Her eyes were closed now, and images from the day ran together. The empty pink and lavender desert. The round eyes of the owl in its round face. The woman's cheek like a withered apple.

Again she saw the outline of the fluteplayer's hump. Again she crossed the Salt River, leapfrogging from stone to stone. Only now the stones were drawings, and she was leaping from picture to picture. She was following them into sleep.

FIVE

May woke at dawn with a bad taste in her mouth. The expression on Evan's face probably mirrored her own.

"It's no dream," she told him as they stared at the breakfast given to them by the girl in the enclosure. The piece of jerky was brown, hard, and nearly unchewable. Soon after, the scar-faced woman came and took the rest of their clothing. In exchange, she gave a deerskin skirt to May, a loincloth to Evan, and a pair of sandals to each. May tried to keep her shirt as well, but the woman refused to let her. May felt intensely embarrassed. She frowned fiercely at the scar-faced woman, who simply ignored her. Then the woman tried to take Evan's glasses, but at this he protested so strongly—and seemed so helpless without them—that she tossed the spectacles back.

Next the children were taken out of the enclosure and set to work picking nuts that grew thick on silvery-green bushes. Dazed, May and Evan did as they were told. When they didn't, the jab of a spear prompted them. Only twice during the day were they allowed water. In the evening they went back inside the enclosure, where the girl shared more food with them: jerky again and a piece of dried meal cake.

Unbelievably, just like that, they had become slaves.

Just like that, they found themselves in a land of villages and campfires and spears. It was not like going back in time, May thought. They were no longer in their own world. They were in a world where men could turn into owls!

FOR A WEEK MAY GATHERED the oily nuts that would be ground up and used to make flour and meal. When she tried to eat one secretly, her mouth puckered and she spat it out. It tasted like aspirin! Later she and the other slave girl were given wooden tongs with which to pick the knobby joints of the cholla cactus. These were covered with fine yellow needles. Picking the cactus was painful until May learned to use the tongs to twist off the joints and lift them, untouched, to a waiting basket. Later she had to rub off the thorns with a stone and roast the joints in a fire.

May had never imagined that life could be so miserable, so dirty, and so uncomfortable. She had never imagined that she could work so hard and eat so little.

At the end of the day, when she and Evan were together, they talked about where they were and why. Sometimes they argued about the man who had turned into an owl. Evan thought that May had simply imagined it. "Shock," he said with a shrug. Mostly they went around and around about the fluteplayer.

"He's the key," Evan would mutter. "That explosion. The sound of that flute . . ."

It was odd, but no matter how much she pitied herself, May pitied Evan even more. As the weeks went by, she could hear him cry with homesickness every night. She knew a little of what he was feeling. She had been homesick herself ever since leaving Philadelphia. Perhaps, she thought, I've used up all my homesickness? Guiltily she wondered why she wasn't more like Evan, why she didn't daydream about her parents and cry for them at night.

Other things just seemed more important now. Water was important, and food, and rest—and freedom. While Evan dreamed of a return to Papago Park, May simply wanted to escape from the village. She wanted to escape from their thorny prison, from the never-ending cycle of chores, from the skimpy meals of dried cake, jerky, and cactus. Above all, she wanted to escape from the dreadful feeling of being owned.

She didn't worry about what they would do afterward. First things first.

"I hate them. I hate them," she would chant to

herself, watching some tribeswomen make a stew of rabbit, wild onion, and a few tender greens. The smell of real food drove her crazy. But the villagers never gave anything like that to slaves.

"It is the painful moon," the other slave girl told May. Her name was Wren, and she used a mixture of gestures and words to communicate. By now May could understand a little of the desert language.

"The painful moon?" she repeated.

"The month before the prickly pear fruit and the rains come," Wren said. "In the summer there will be plenty for all of us."

After nearly three weeks, May knew the other slave children very well. Wren was the sweet one. About ten years old—two years younger than May— she had a heart-shaped face and yellow, almond-shaped eyes. Quick and brown, she flitted about the enclosure exactly like a wren in a tree. The older boy, Horn, seemed her opposite—heavy where Wren was light and sullen where she was cheerful. The youngest of them was called Pointer. He was a sal-low imp about seven years old, whose chin and nose jutted out comically. Full of mischief, Pointer often made the tribespeople roar with laughter at his jokes and antics.

As that first month passed and the "painful moon" came to an end, May and Evan learned more of the desert language. While Evan went with the other boys, May and Wren often worked together, picking and gathering and talking softly. As long as the slaves kept a steady pace, the villagers did not mind if the obedient Wren taught the new girl.

THE SCAR-FACED WOMAN was in charge on the day May returned to the river. Because it marked the edge of their territory, the tribe feared the river and did not go there often. Instead they used a small spring near the village. At times, however, the women needed running water to soften the leaves of the yucca plant they sometimes used for clothing. It was on one such trip, as they pounded and rinsed and pounded and rinsed, that Wren told May about the six tribes.

Each tribe was named for a different desert animal.

"Each has its own magic," Wren said. Together they knelt on the riverbank. Once again, bubbling water rushed past May with a pleasant sound. "But you already know that."

"No, I don't. Tell me!"

Wren's face assumed the humoring expression she often gave seven-year-old Pointer.

"Please, Wren," May begged.

Patiently Wren began.

The first tribe were their masters, the Javelinas, named for the hairy wild pig of the desert, with its sharp, spearlike tusks. The Javelinas could direct the summer rains. They moved the clouds and brought down their moisture on the saguaro fields. In the fall the tribe searched for roots and small game. In the winter they often went hungry. But in the summer, ah, they called the rain and feasted on lovely, rich, ripe saguaro fruit. Then they grew fat and happy.

"Move the clouds?" May scoffed.

"It is their power," Wren said with a shrug. "When the rains come, you'll see."

Across from the Javelinas, north across the river, lived the Owl tribe. They could fly through the air.

"Yes, yes!" May said, forgetting to work in her excitement. "I saw one of them. I saw him fly!"

"The Owls fly," Wren agreed matter-of-factly. "They are the most powerful of all the tribes. They eat sand and drink the blood of children. Everyone fears them."

May nodded, storing this away to tell Evan.

Wren continued serenely.

To the west, on the other side of the Owls, were the curly-haired, golden-skinned, blue-eyed Sheep tribe, whose people could put their ears to the earth, listen to it, and make things grow. They planted seeds from which marvelous foods sprung, and they built great towns to store their harvest. Horn was a Sheep, and like him, they were a strong, slow people. Like the bighorn sheep, they loved to climb high into the nearby mountains. From these rocky perches they could look across the desert plains—farther north still, to where the land was forbidden, taboo, empty of people and full of monsters.

South and west of the Javelinas the timid Packrats thrived in the most barren part of the desert world. They were a small people who had the magic ability to walk for days without drink or food. Although they were poor, they made beautiful baskets decorated with the designs of flowers and stars.

Finally, east of the Packrats lived the tawny-skinned Pumas—hunters with the strength and speed of the mountain lion. They ate only meat and taught their children to kill running deer with their bare hands. The Pumas could understand the wordless thoughts of animals. Sometimes they befriended a wolf or a bear or a mountain lion itself. More often they used their power to track down a luckless rabbit or badger.

"Their eyes are green as grass," Wren whispered. "Their teeth are very sharp."

The last tribe, the sixth, were the yellow Coyotes. They roamed throughout the desert in small bands. Pointer belonged to this mischievous tribe, who had no homeland of their own. Instead they were petty thieves and musicians and traders—and the inventors of clever toys. "Like the clothes you wore and those funny sandals," Wren said.

"No," May interrupted. "The Coyotes didn't make those."

Wren ignored this. She lifted her mass of wet yucca leaves onto a rock. May did the same, using a stone to scrape away the softened pulp.

"And what is the Coyotes' magic?" May asked.

Wren looked uneasy. "The Coyotes have secrets" was all she would say.

May was already thinking of another question. "And the fluteplayer we saw in the cave?" she probed cautiously. "Who is he? Where does he belong?"

Using a stick in the sand, Evan had already drawn the fluteplayer for the other children. They had responded oddly. Wren had looked quickly away and Horn had rubbed the picture out. Then they had refused to talk about it. The Javelinas had been more direct. As soon as Evan drew the rounded hump, the tribespeople jumped on the boy, pushed him down, and bloodied his nose.

Now Wren shook her head vigorously. A Javelina woman glared at them.

"Well, then, what about me?" May tried. "Where do you think I come from, Wren?"

Her friend's back arched as she pounded the pointed leaves with a stone. May had learned to wait through these silences, sometimes necessary because of the work. She bent too, sweating and rebellious. She wondered why the desert people were so incurious about her and Evan. No one asked about *her* tribe or fussed over Evan's red hair. No one seemed to care where they came from.

I don't think they really see us, May thought. They just make use of us. Poof. Magic. Two new slaves.

Where does Wren belong? May asked herself.

She's not an Owl or a Puma. She's not a Javelina or a Sheep or a Coyote. Is she a Packrat?

But Wren was speaking. "I think you are like me," she said in a low voice. "You have no tribe."

"Of course I do." May stopped her work. "I'm an American."

Wren looked at her as though she hadn't heard. There was pity in her look, and something else. "I thought I was the only one," she went on hurriedly. May had never seen the other girl so upset. "None of the other tribes look like me. I have no tribe. I belong nowhere." Wren kept pounding harder at her mass of yucca leaves. "You and Evan are like me!" she said again. "You belong nowhere!"

She hid her face in embarrassment.

"But Wren." May tried to be gentle. "That doesn't make sense. You're as real as I am. There must be a seventh tribe."

Wren gave a startled burst of laughter. "There are only six tribes," she said with certainty.

"But Wren!" Now May couldn't help feeling irritated. "You do exist. Right? You're here! You should be trying to find out who you are. Maybe you come from my world. You should be trying to find out where your tribe is. You should . . ."

Her voice trailed away. What could Wren do—really? What could any of them do, locked up behind ocotillo thorns, enslaved in the middle of the burning desert?

Thinking about it later, May decided that Wren's

face had shown only relief when the scar-faced woman chose that moment to come over and scold them.

First the woman slapped Wren on the cheek. "Get to work!" she screeched unfairly.

Then she turned to May. "As for you, little queen. Oh, queen, queen, come to us!" She pantomimed the scene in which the two spearmen had convinced May and Evan to cross the river. All the Javelinas thought this a very good joke. Blushing, May was reminded of her classmates back in Phoenix.

"Can't you do anything right?" The Javelina grabbed May's stone to demonstrate the correct scraping technique. She winked at the others. "Here, so, like this. Careful! Or we'll give you to the Owls! They eat sand and drink the blood of children! They'll eat you alive!"

The women chuckled. Then, remembering where they were, they looked anxiously across the flowing water.

SIX

That night, as usual, May and Evan made their beds apart from the other children. This was the time, snatched before sleep, when they could exchange news. Now May told Evan about the six tribes.

"Weird," Evan said, wiggling to get comfortable on the hard ground.

"Six kinds of magic," May mused.

"Well . . ." Evan was still doubtful about that.

"Don't you believe Wren?" May protested.

"Sure I do. At least about the six different tribes. When you look at Horn and Pointer and the Javelinas, they *do* seem genetically different, like three different races."

"If only Wren had some kind of magic," May said half to herself. "Maybe we could use it to help us escape."

Evan ignored this. "It's convenient," he noted, "that they all speak the same language. Pointer was mimicking Horn's accent today. The Javelina men were in hysterics."

"Was Horn mad?"

"No, I've never seen Horn mad."

"I've never seen him feel anything," May complained. "He doesn't have any emotions at all."

"It's the way his people are." Evan put on his teaching voice. "They believe that once a Sheep got so angry he almost destroyed the entire tribe. Now they try to stay calm. Horn won't rush his work, you know, even when a Javelina is yelling at him. He has a lot of dignity."

May knew how much Evan admired the older boy.

"Yeah, so how did he get here anyway?" she asked. "Did he calmly, with dignity, allow himself to be carried off?"

"He got lost," Evan told her. "He was only five, climbing a mountain when the Javelinas caught him in a trap."

"Then he's been here for years!"

"Over ten. Soon after he came, they brought Wren. She was just a baby. A woman nursed her, and then Horn took over."

"And Wren can remember when Pointer came a year ago." May shook her head. "Pointer says his mother traded him for something the Javelinas had. Imagine trading away your own son! Pointer says his mother is a leader in his tribe, a big chief."

Now it was Evan's turn to be sarcastic. "If you can believe what *Pointer* says."

Smiling, May stared up at the Milky Way. The glittering sweep of stars filled the sky. She remembered the night skies she had seen in Phoenix and Philadelphia, with their pale pinpricks of light. It seemed to her that she had never really seen stars until she came here. Now she only wished that the ocotillo fence were not there to interrupt her view.

If only we were free, May thought. If only I could see the whole sky! She whispered again to Evan. "What does Horn say about Pointer?"

"He says Pointer just appeared one morning, like a fleabite. You should have seen Horn this afternoon!" Evan burst out suddenly with pride. "We were digging the floor for a storage hut, and I was awfully thirsty. But the Javelinas wouldn't give us any water. Then Horn stood up to them. He said he wouldn't dig until they got me a drink! A Javelina came over to hit us, and Horn just stared at him. The Javelina got us some water *fast*. Horn's as strong as two men."

May said nothing. Then she came up on one arm. As strong as two men? It took two men to roll the stone away from the fence's gate . . .

"Is he strong enough to push away that boulder?" she asked. "Of course he'd have to be outside . . ."

Evan sat up too. "Listen, May, before you make any plans. I've talked to Horn. He won't help. He doesn't want to leave here."

But May was thinking furiously.

"May!" Evan said. "I work with him, and I

know one thing. You can't push Horn around. Don't get bossy."

"Bossy?" May huffed.

"Remember." Evan lay back down. "I want to get out of here as much as you do. We've got to get back to that cave and the picture of the fluteplayer. It's the key somehow . . ."

"But if Horn could only . . ." May began.

It was Evan's turn not to listen.

He's thinking about Phoenix, May thought. He's thinking about his brother who plays the saxophone.

Evan lay still.

May knew enough now to leave him alone.

ALL THE NEXT MORNING and afternoon May thought about her new plan of escape. Meanwhile, the Javelinas seemed excited about something and stopped their work early. Back in the enclosure May watched the others as they ate together in the late afternoon light. Finally she stood up with a flourish and called for their attention.

"Next month," she began, "we start harvesting the saguaro cactus."

Wren nodded. Evan looked at May suspiciously. Pointer clapped his hands, prepared to laugh and cheer her on. Horn only blinked—already half asleep.

"Wren says that the Javelinas boil the saguaro fruit and make a drink and on a special night they have a big feast and everyone has a lot and they all get drunk." May paused for breath.

"They give us some, too," Pointer told her. "Everyone gets to drink."

"Yes," May said. She had prepared a careful speech, but now she found herself rushing through the words. "Only we don't have to drink it. We can stay awake, and Horn can push away the boulder, and we can escape that night!"

In her hurry she had left out the important part. "I mean we'll scrape off the thorns from the gate and he can push away the boulder from the inside!"

May almost danced with how simple it was. Evan glowered at her, but she went on. "The Javelinas won't notice that we're gone because they'll be so drunk! They'll come after us the next morning, but by that time we'll be across the river."

"Across the river?" Pointer yipped. "The Owls live there!"

"Yes, we'll be on their land. But we'll hide from them."

"Hide from the Owls?" asked Pointer doubtfully.

"Why not? They won't be expecting us."

"I don't know if that matters," Wren said softly.

"It might," May argued. "Anyway, we won't be there long. We'll travel on to Horn's tribe."

The Sheep's curly-haired head jerked up at this.

"Hey!" Evan protested.

"Oh, we'll stop at the cave to see the flute-player," May assured him. "If nothing happens there, we'll go *looking* for him! We'll help Horn find his tribe. And Pointer find his. And Wren . . ."

May stopped because Horn was standing now,

and Horn looked very tall. May knew that talking about where Wren came from was another taboo subject—like the fluteplayer or the mention of escape. The three desert children didn't want to talk about these things. They didn't want to think about them. Defiantly May faced the Sheep.

Maybe I am bossy, she thought. But maybe that's exactly what they need.

"And then we'll help Wren find her tribe," May said loudly. "She has to come from somewhere!"

May pushed back the unruly mess of her brown hair, dirty and uncombed. Horn and Evan were both furious, she knew, and Pointer looked uncertain, torn between fear and his love of adventure. But suddenly it was only Wren who mattered. It was Wren who bent her head and refused to look up.

"I'm not being selfish!" May cried. "This is for you, Wren, most of all. You have to find out who you are! Aren't you curious? Don't you want to find your own tribe? Oh, you can't be happy here!" The words came straight from May's heart. "You can't be happy being owned, never free to do anything, to take a walk or talk to a friend. Why won't you even try to leave? Just try!"

With a feeling of rightness she met Horn's eyes. For a moment she thought she had won.

Then Wren spoke. "Well, someone did try once."

Horn exhaled, and his big body slumped with exhaustion. He had worked most of the day digging pits for roasting.

"Before Pointer came," Wren said, her voice ris-

ing, "there was another little boy from the Puma
tribe. He also hated this place. He hated the work
and being owned, as you say. He fought with the
Javelinas and with us, too, pacing up and down every
night. One night he jumped over the fence."

"He jumped *over* the fence?" Evan repeated. The
fence was at least six feet tall.

"They brought in his body to show us," Horn
said, taking up the story. "A Javelina speared him on
the other side. A Javelina is there tonight, watching
and waiting. Do you think they leave the enclosure
and us unguarded? No, not even on a festival night."

"You never told me that before," Pointer complained.

"You never thought of leaving before," Horn replied.

Slowly May sat down.

"Just push the boulder away." Horn's words
came out measured and hard, like thrown rocks.
"But it is not so easy. Cross the river into the land
of the flying Owls! It is not that simple. Even if this
could be done, even if we could find my tribe, what
then? *The tribes do not mix.* Where would Wren go?
No one will accept her. She has no tribe. Neither do
you! Could you survive, alone, without a tribe, in
the desert?"

"Here we have enough to eat and drink," Wren
pleaded. "What more do you want?"

May imagined the body of the little Puma boy in
frightening detail. She felt stunned. Horn was right.
It was not so easy.

SEVEN

The next morning the children hardly spoke. Silently they ate a breakfast of the newly ripe prickly pear fruit. Then the boys were sent to dig and the girls to gather. As May and Wren filled their baskets, they saw a group of Javelinas join in a circle nearby.

"Watch their spears," Wren whispered to May.

The Javelinas, six men and six women, stood with their backs to one another. One by one they threw long sharpened sticks into the air. May watched closely. The spears flew up—and disappeared. May squinted and looked harder. But the spears never came down.

One by one, to the south and to the west, scattered clouds began to move toward the knot of tribespeople. Puffs of fluffy white sailed over May's head, and she stared up in amazement. The clouds came as though they were being called! As they merged together, they turned grayer and darker.

"Now it will rain," Wren said with satisfaction, "where the Javelinas want it to rain."

But even as the girls watched, the mass of clouds sped toward the Javelinas and then went past them, on and on, like ships out to the desert sea. The Javelinas murmured with anger and fear.

"What's happening?" May asked Wren.

"I don't know!" Wren said. "But the clouds did not obey. I don't know why."

Whatever was happening, it put the Javelinas in a very bad mood.

The very next day five tribesmen held the Sheep slave boy down while a sixth took a knife and cut partially through the tendon on Horn's right ankle. Immediately after, the Javelinas packed the cut with a pasty mass of leaves so that the wound would not infect. When they let Horn up, he took a step and fell. For the rest of his life his right foot would be a weight to be dragged, pushed, and lifted.

Now Horn moved like an old man, which satisfied the Javelinas. Although the other children were deeply shocked, the Sheep himself never complained.

"Why did they do it?" May asked Evan in despair. "You don't think that they heard me . . . when I talked about Horn and the boulder?"

"No." Evan shook his head. "They were scared before that. Remember the day when he made them get me water? They needed an advantage over him."

"It's so horrible!"

"The Romans did the same thing to their slaves."

May stared up at another perfect starry night. "You were right about one thing," she said hopelessly. "He'll never leave. He's accepted this like everything else. He doesn't care what they do to him."

"No," Evan agreed. His shaky voice, full of tears, grew suddenly clear. "But Wren does."

This, May realized, was true.

Now began the time of the saguaro harvest, and the days passed in a blur of work. Horn's cut healed quickly, although the limp remained. Each night when the Sheep came back from work, Wren had to look away from his dragging foot. Her heart-shaped face grew pinched. Sudden storms flickered behind her yellow eyes. Once May caught her staring north, her entire body trembling. Once, at night, she talked a babble of nonsense in her sleep. She never mentioned the subject of leaving or of finding her own tribe. Yet May sensed that something was growing deep inside Wren, something that fell between anger and hope.

EIGHT

O nce the harvest began, May came to know
the saguaro as she had never known a plant before.
She knew its smooth trunk that divided into ridges,
on each ridge a line of sharp needles. She knew the
cactus wren that dug nests into the saguaro's flesh.
She learned to watch for scorpions at the plant's
thorny base. Like the others, she waited eagerly for
her share of its rich, sweet fruit. That purple fruit!
Nothing had ever tasted so good.

Young and old, everyone in the tribe worked at
the harvest. While the men poked at the top of a
high cactus with a pole, the women and children
gathered what fell below. On the ground they split
the fruit that had not yet broken, scooping out the
red pulp and discarding the prickly outer shell. Later
the pulp would be soaked overnight to remove its
black seeds, which were ground into a fine flour for
cakes.

The Javelinas continued to try their rain magic.

And it continued to be unpredictable. Sometimes the saguaro fields were drenched by a shower. Sometimes the clouds swept over the tribe to drop their burden on another part of the desert. The summer rains had come—but for the first time, Wren told May, the Javelinas could not control them.

Evan didn't believe in the Javelinas' magic. "It must have been a trick of the light," he insisted when May described how the spears had disappeared.

Both he and May watched as the best of the saguaro pulp was boiled until it looked like a dark liquid jam. This was poured into a clay jar, sealed with yellow mud, and buried in the ground. There, Pointer said, the syrup would change into a fiery alcoholic drink.

"It makes you very sick." The boy grinned. "We'll take the jars out on the night of the festival. Everyone will get sick and start dancing until they fall down! It's a good time when the saguaro fruit comes."

Maybe I'm crazy, May thought, but it *is* a good time!

Although the older Javelinas were angry over the failure of their magic, the young ones enjoyed the harvest as usual—the boys flirting with girls and the girls flirting back. Everyone had a full stomach. Along with the saguaro fruit there were also lamb's-quarter leaves, mesquite beans, and inch-long worms that the Javelinas prized but that May and Evan refused to eat. It was May's first summer in the desert, and she saw with wonder how the rains greened the hills and washed the sky of dust. The rains brought life; they *were* life.

Now, in an odd turnabout, she looked forward to going to work with the Javelinas. At least it was better than being left alone with the other slaves. Horn's silence had grown until it was a well deep enough to drown in. His awkward limp made them all feel sad. Evan suffered through a new and severe bout of homesickness. Pointer moped because Wren wouldn't play with him. Wren just sat and stared at the ocotillo fence, intent on her own thoughts.

By the time Wren finally spoke about trying to escape, the five children knew that the girl was only saying what they had already come to accept.

"Someday they may cripple us all, Horn. Not just you. We must leave on the night of the festival." Wren was standing before them as May had done earlier.

"I can't go like this," the Sheep mumbled.

"Even now," Wren scoffed, "you are stronger than any of us."

"What about the fence?" Horn asked.

"You can push the boulder away."

"And the guards?" he persisted.

The children stirred uneasily.

"Everyone will be drunk," Pointer said. "There won't be any guards!"

Horn shook his head. "There will be at least one, someone out of favor with the chief."

"We must overpower him." Wren sounded calm. "Then we can tie and gag him."

May felt frightened. Five children against one or perhaps two adults with spears? Evan looked at her as though to say, "Are you happy now? Is this what you wanted?"

"What will we do afterward?" Horn pressed.

"We'll cross the river to the land of the Owls," Wren said. "We'll hide from them and walk to Sheep land."

"And then?"

"And then we'll see what happens."

Horn was silent.

"When is the festival, anyway?" May asked.

She was hardly prepared for the answer.

"When?" Pointer laughed. "Tomorrow! Didn't you know? Tomorrow is the night of our escape."

ALL THE NEXT DAY the Javelinas bustled about with preparations. First the women and men used red and white clay to paint themselves with geometric designs. Then food had to be made and a special shelter built of mesquite poles and yucca thatch. The Javelinas kept their slaves busy until early evening, when the children were handed a gourd of fermented saguaro juice and shoved back into the enclosure. May and Evan tasted the drink before Wren poured it out.

"Bleah!" May wiped her mouth in disgust.

Later all the Javelinas began to shake their gourd rattles and dance and sing. Unexpectedly, Pointer joined them with a high, sweet soprano. Evan raised an eyebrow at May as the grubby little boy was transformed into a choir angel.

"Enough," Horn said at last. "We don't want attention."

May wished that Horn could silence the Javelinas as easily. In bursts of drunken excitement, loud, harsh, wild, and out-of-tune, the villagers filled the night with their roars. They'll *never* stop, May thought.

Despite the noise, she found herself fighting sleep. Then, after what seemed but a second later, she felt Horn's hand on her shoulder. May jerked awake. The hills were already glowing pink.

"Hurry!" urged Horn, moving on to Pointer.

"But it's light!" May protested.

"They've been quiet for an hour," Evan told her. "We're about to call the guard."

The children stood by the prickly gate. There was nothing to pack and no one to say good-bye to. Wren picked up the gourd they had emptied of saguaro juice. They would fill it up with water at the river. In the gray dawn Evan's freckles stood out. He began to yell. "Help! Help! A scorpion! Wren's been bit by a scorpion!"

He had to call a long time before the guard shuffled over. "I can't move the stone alone," the Javelina bellowed through the fence. "And no one will get up now! You'll have to wait." The man sounded angry.

"But she's sick! She'll die!" Evan cried.

"We can't wait," Horn said. "You don't want to lose a good slave, do you? Not while you're on duty! *I'll* move the stone."

"No one will get up now," the confused guard repeated.

Horn had already put his shoulder against the ocotillo gate. Earlier Wren had tried to scrape the thorns away, but drops of blood still ran down the Sheep's golden skin. May could hear the fence branches crack apart as he pushed with all his might. Muttering, the Javelina guard stood by. Horn's face screwed into a fearful mask. His arm muscles bunched into knots and sweat mingled with the blood on his arm. He grunted before giving one tremendous final shove.

The stone rolled. The gate swung open. But the guard did not come in.

"Huh!" the Javelina snorted. "The new boy-slave can come out carrying the girl. No one else! Anyone else will be speared!"

"Go on," Horn said very low to Evan. "I'll be right behind you. Get hold of his spear if you can."

Wren groaned convincingly as Evan grabbed her under the arms and dragged her through the opening. May heard the guard say something. Suddenly Evan yelped, and the space where Horn had been standing was empty. Then May leaped through the open gate, landing on the guard's leg. The earth smelled of vomit and sour alcohol. Clenching her teeth, May managed to keep from crying out as the leg beneath her kicked and bucked. To the side she could see Evan pinning the Javelina's arm. Horn smashed his fist against the guard's temple. Abruptly the man was still.

"Find some rope," Horn hissed at Pointer.

They tied up the Javelina and gagged him with long yucca leaves. Already the outline of the hills showed plainly against the sky. By the time they were halfway to the river the sun would be shining full on the village. The women would be waking to the cries of hungry babies. The men would rise reluctantly from their places on the ground. Then when the guard and missing slaves were discovered, the men would put their best runners on the trail.

"What about knives and food?" Evan gasped.

"There's no time!" Wren sounded shrill.

"No time!" May repeated. She found it hard to breathe. The silence of the village frightened her. Her own freedom frightened her, and panic rose like a dark liquid in her throat.

"Let's go!" she cried.

"Yes, we must go!"

They turned and hurried down the faint path to the river. Horn led the way, his long legs making up for his limp.

NINE

As the water sparkled white in the sun, May and Evan stood once again in the middle of the rushing Salt River. This time they did not hesitate. Already behind them an angry Javelina appeared on the crest of a hill. May thought she heard a spear thunk nearby. But she never really knew, for she was too busy splashing to the river's other bank. The scenery blurred as she followed Evan up a hill, around a mesquite bush, through a dry arroyo, deeper and deeper into the land of the Owls. Finally Pointer fell and would not get up. May stopped gratefully beside the boy. Her chest was on fire. She bent over. Through the sound of her own breathing she could hear Evan wheeze.

Horn had also dropped to the ground.

"The Javelinas won't go past the river," Wren said. Oddly, the girl hardly panted. Her body seemed made for the swiftness of flight. "The Owls are our worry now. And water."

At the very word May felt thirsty. They had meant to fill their gourd at the river. "Can't we go back?" she asked.

"We could," Wren answered. "But I think the Javelinas will be there waiting for us. They'll have their spears."

Horn stood up slowly, favoring his bad ankle. "Better to go on," he agreed.

Nervously they all looked north. The buzz of a fly sounded like an alarm in May's ears. The land of the Owls screamed "Intruder!" The rocks watched them with hidden eyes. The breeze carried their scent.

"If we don't go back for water, I know what that means." Pointer said too loudly.

"Yes." Wren smiled at him. "We must find a barrel cactus. We can cut off the top," she explained to May and Evan, "and pound the inside for liquid. It's a bitter drink."

"The cave is only a few hours away," Evan reminded Horn. "We have to go there first!"

The Sheep nodded and set off, his limp more obvious than before.

To May's surprise the trip to the cave seemed short. She remembered the first time that she had walked these hills, with the prickly pear rearing up dagger-sharp to catch her. Now, though they had been traveling since dawn, she kept the pace easily. This time, she was glad to be wearing so little—her sandaled feet light on the sand and her legs strong. It seemed like no time at all before she recognized the hill ahead with its humped granite peak.

With Evan in the lead they passed the spot where the class had eaten their lunch. Only May and Evan knew that in another world a fountain would be there with a spray of cold water. In another, very different world there were benches to sit on and a city nearby.

Evan looked at her meaningfully. In her mind's eye May saw him as he had been before—the popular, confident boy so neatly dressed in blue jeans and a white T-shirt. Now his red hair hung jagged to his shoulders. One by one she could count the ribs on his chest. As he scrambled up the hill, May knew what he was thinking. He was thinking that soon all their problems might be over. He was thinking that the fluteplayer had brought them here, and the fluteplayer could take them back.

"Come on!" Evan whispered, and rushed ahead to the cave's entrance. There his back straightened unnaturally and his hand froze in midair. "That's crazy," he said. "That's impossible."

May pushed past him through the opening, her eyes squinting in the dim light.

"Quiet!" Horn cautioned as he entered the cave. The big Sheep looked about in approval while Wren and Pointer crowded in behind. The cave held them tightly in its stony embrace.

Only Evan stayed outside in the heat of the afternoon sun.

Once again May went to touch the far wall. The rock felt cold to her fingers and slightly gritty. Only this time she could see no mark or outline. There was no picture of a hump rising above a skinny neck. No drawing of a flute. No mocking smile. May felt as empty as the wall before her. The fluteplayer was gone as though he had never existed.

AFTER A BRIEF REST, Horn gave them their assignments.

"Work!" May complained. "I thought we were done with that."

Wren laughed. In the desert the work of finding food and water was never done. May, Evan, and Horn went out to break open a barrel cactus while Wren and Pointer gathered a meal of saguaro fruit and mesquite beans. May was worried about Evan. Silently he did as he was told. But his movements were slow, and under a fiery sunburn his face looked greenish.

"Listen," she said to him as they cut at one side of a cactus with rocks. She paused. She didn't know why the fluteplayer was gone or how they would ever get back to Phoenix. Part of her didn't even care. Like Horn, she wanted only to return to the cave and hide until daylight had passed. She wanted some saguaro fruit and a drink of water. Above all, like a song humming through her veins, she thrilled to a new sense of liberty and competence. They had done it! They were free!

"Listen," May began again. "There are plenty of explanations for this. There's no use thinking the worst."

Evan dropped his rock and turned on her. "Speak English!" he yelled. "You don't even speak English anymore!"

"Quiet," Horn commanded sternly. With one swing of his jagged rock he chopped at the base of the cactus so that the plant jerked and toppled over. "Here." Horn hastily cut away some of the thorns. "Help me carry this back to the cave."

For the rest of the afternoon they took turns napping and pounding the pulpy flesh of the barrel cactus. Wren was right. The drops of liquid they got tasted awful. But May was too wise now to spit out her first mouthful. She swallowed and grimaced. "Can we live on this?" she asked Wren. "Can't we go back to the river?"

The others were awake. It was a good time to talk. Wren doled out a handful of curvy mesquite bean pods to each of them. Eaten raw, the pods tasted sweet and crunchy. Outside the cave, shadows lengthened as the sun moved west. Inside, the children felt cool and sheltered.

"I don't think we should travel by the river,"

Horn said. "That may be where the Owls get their water. The Javelinas will be watching it as well."

"Where are we going exactly?" May felt lost.

With the end of a mesquite pod Horn drew a picture on the dirt floor. "Like the Javelinas, the Sheep are separated from the Owls by water. To reach this stream we must go west through the desert. Then we cross these mountains, here. After that, it is a short walk to my village." Horn made a small circle in the dirt. He smiled, looking oddly relaxed.

There's something about this cave that makes us all feel good, May thought. Without prompting, Horn chatted on about his tribe. Wren looked confident and happy as she squeezed a piece of barrel cactus. Pointer snuggled into a sleepy ball. May tried to see Evan's face. Did he feel it too? Did he feel that sense of safety and protection, as though the fluteplayer were still here—a guardian spirit watching over them?

"When do we start?" Evan asked.

"When the moon comes up," Horn replied. "We're lucky to have the light. Without water we cannot go during the day."

"Night is best for the Owls too," Wren warned.

May recalled the man and then the bird: the white disklike face, the curved beak, the talons.

"We should sleep now," Horn said dreamily. "Soon enough we will find my people. We will find the Sheep."

TEN

They started under a full moon, and for all the nights of their traveling the desert was gilded with its eerie glow. The plants and rocks shone yellow, silver, and white. The winds blew warm. The sky was cloudless.

"The rains have ended early," Horn said. Disturbed, he and Wren looked at each other. Horn was leading the way. His right foot dragged, but he stepped eagerly as he followed his instincts west to the Sheep tribe. Wren walked behind him, then Pointer, Evan, and May.

It was Evan who slowed them down. His fair skin was sensitive, and at the Javelina village he had been careful to protect it with mud and leaves. On the morning of their escape, however, they had left too quickly for that. Now, after their flight to the river and cave, his back and shoulders were badly blistered.

May walked behind him and felt guiltier than ever. Evan suffered, and she was happy! It seemed that she and Evan were changing places in this strange land. He was discovering within himself a new vulnerability, while she was finding new strengths. More than this, she was learning about the desert, which seemed more beautiful to her each day. She had never seen anything like these moonlit nights with their long stretches of stars, rock, and cactus. Intoxicated, she felt like a deer skimming over the earth, like a bird flying through canyons of air, like a snake sidling along the desert floor.

"I could walk forever," she said to herself.

On the second day the children slept under the shade of a large mesquite tree. May woke in the afternoon to see three Owls flying above her. Their great wings flapped. Their beaked faces turned this way and that. In a panic May shook Wren's shoulder. Immediately the girl opened her eyes.

"They don't like to be out in the daylight," Wren whispered as she peered carefully through the mesquite branches. "They're searching for us. Or perhaps they carry a message."

Wren seemed very sure of this. As she watched the Owls disappear, she almost seemed to smile in triumph.

May also stared up at the deep-blue sky, streaked with a single wisp of cloud. As a slave, Wren had always been obedient and timid. She had been the one who wanted only to please, the one the Javelinas trusted to behave. She had seemed to be the kind of girl who would always follow and never lead.

May knew better now.

"They won't return," Wren told her.

"I'm worried about Evan." May kept her voice low. "He's so hot. He needs more water."

They had scooped out a hole for Evan, digging away the sandy gravel until they reached a layer of cooler soil. He lay there now, his back protected by the few green leaves they could find. The mesquite tree kept them hidden from the sun—and from the Owls as well, May realized gratefully. The curvy tan mesquite pods hung above them like so many Christmas decorations. On the ground the crushed beans sent out a sweet scent.

Wren reached over to touch Evan's forehead. Her fingers brushed his skin, and her face tightened.

"If only we could find a spring!" May exclaimed. The barrel cactus they depended on were becoming harder to find. They seemed to grow in groups throughout the desert and then disappear for long stretches. "Or some saguaro fruit," May went on. She sat up to scan the horizon for the tall cactus.

"Yes," Wren murmured. "But all the saguaro fruit has been picked. You can see the empty shells."

"It's the Owls," May reminded her. "Horn found one of the poles they use to bring down the fruit. Remember?"

"Yes," Wren said in an odd tone. "The Owls harvest the saguaro just like the Javelinas. I thought they ate blood and sand! I thought they would have found us on that first night!"

"Maybe the Owls aren't as scary as you thought they were," May suggested.

"Yes," Wren murmured again. "Maybe nothing is the way I thought it was."

The afternoon heat wrapped around them like a too-warm blanket choking their thoughts and breath. May slept again and at twilight woke to find Horn squeezing a broken barrel cactus. He let its liquid dribble into the gourd Wren had brought from the Javelina village.

"That's all we have." Horn shrugged. "We must find another one tonight. As we walk, Pointer and I will look to the right. You three look to the left."

"We'll find one," Wren promised.

But they didn't.

May soon forgot that she had ever been happy walking through the silver desert. Her throat hurt when she spoke or swallowed, her lips cracked, and the skin on her arms peeled away in dry strips. Her walk became an exhausted shuffle. By the fourth night it was obvious that Evan could not do even that. His body burned with fever and shook with chills. That day, they could not find a tree or rock large enough to sleep under and were forced to build a shelter out of creosote brush. This time when night fell and they had to move on, only Horn and Wren stood up. The others lay where they were.

Dimly May heard Horn's voice.

"We're almost at the base of the mountains. If I hurry, I can reach the stream that separates Owl and Sheep before morning. I can come back with water."

"Let me go," Wren said.

Horn said something that sounded angry.

Evan's eyes were closed. May wondered if he understood what was happening. "Wait," she whispered into his ear. "Horn is going to get us water."

She could see Horn standing now, the gourd a shadow in his hand. He hesitated, and May understood that he was afraid. For ten years he had never been alone. A Javelina or Pointer or Wren had always kept him company.

"Don't come back to us in the day," Wren warned him. "Don't risk the heat. We can wait."

May fell asleep then. Although she had rested all day, she slept again through most of the night. At some point, in the darkness, Evan crawled out of the crowded shelter. By the time May and Wren dragged him back in it was late morning, and he had spent hours under the hot sun. His tongue was nearly black, his face pale.

They waited all that day. Forced to squeeze together under the thin shade, their sweat mingled and their limbs grew cramped. Heat rashes covered May's neck and chest, and when the muscles in her calves tightened, she kicked the others in her haste to stretch. Mercifully, Evan lay asleep or unconscious. But May found that she was painfully awake.

First there was the fire in her throat.

Then she began to imagine strange things. A scorpion wiggled in her hair and whispered to her. She reached to grab it and instead touched the shell of a saguaro fruit filled with owl feathers. Terrified, May begged Wren to let them return to the Javelina village.

When she was thinking more clearly, May remembered that Horn was coming back with water that night! She caught Pointer's eye and tried to speak to him through cracked lips. Night fell again, and she sank into its forgetfulness.

When May woke, the diamond sun glared in the sky as though it had never left. Still Horn had not come. Fear gave May the energy to sit up. Perhaps if she searched, she would find a saguaro or a green spring shining in the desert. But when she tried to crawl out of the shelter, her arms collapsed and she fell on Pointer. The boy's eyes barely flickered.

"Evan?" May whispered. Evan, too, gave no response. May noticed then that the shelter seemed roomier. She struggled to her knees. Horn's never coming back. The words formed clearly in her mind. She tried to speak but couldn't. "Wren! Wren!" she mouthed.

But now Wren was gone as well.

After that, May never knew how many days or nights passed, or if any passed at all.

She remembered only a dream of the fluteplayer standing tall and slender and forcing a spear down her throat.

"It's for your own good!" The fluteplayer sneered.

May struggled as she felt the sharp blade touch her lips.

Then suddenly the spear turned into a stream of ice-cold lemonade.

Then the stream was warm, and the spear flowed like a ribbon of blood.

Then there was no spear at all, only the sun seen red through her closed eyes.

The blood was river water.

And the fluteplayer was Wren, her heart-shaped face tired and worried.

PART TWO

THE
GATHERING
OF TRIBES

ELEVEN

May rested by the gently rushing stream. Evan lay nearby, under the shade of a cottonwood tree, his back and legs lapped by water. When he woke, the stream had cooled his fever enough for him to sit up and croak, "I can't see! I can't see!"

"Wait a second. I've got them here." Awkwardly May fitted his eyeglasses to his sunburned nose. She had carried these glasses for most of that dreadful, delirious trip.

Instead of saying thank you, Evan only grabbed the ends irritably and set them right. Then he fastened the elastic sports band around his head.

Knee-deep in the water, Pointer gave May a toothy grin. Wren was out gathering food. Horn slept motionless on the stream bank.

"How do you feel?" May asked Evan. She squatted comfortably beside him.

"Uh," he grunted. He stood up and looked

around. The stream was small, lined with patches of grass and surrounded by saguaro, mesquite, and giant buckhorn cholla. Evan stared at a rise of hills that rose jagged into the sky.

"We've been traveling west," he said slowly. "If we were home, we'd be just a few miles west of Phoenix, south of the town Wickenburg."

May didn't know what to say. Of course there was no Wickenburg here. No Phoenix. No home.

"What happened?" Evan turned to her. The movement made him wince. "Did Horn carry me here?"

"No." May's eyes flickered to the Sheep boy on the ground. "Horn didn't make it to the stream. He got close and then he collapsed. Heat exhaustion, I think. Wren went to get us water."

"Wren brought us water," Pointer put in. "I carried you!"

"Well, we all did." May smiled. "Actually, you walked most of the way. Then we found Horn and helped him here too."

"I carried Horn!" Pointer said ridiculously.

May waded into the stream to splash the little boy. It was nearly evening, the air almost cool. In the distance a quail called *who are you? who are you?* as the sky put on a glorious show of red and orange.

"Hurray! We're safe now!" May shouted impulsively. "We're on Sheep land. We made it past the Owls!"

"We made it!" Pointer cried.

"You silly birds!" May yelled.

She threw water at Evan, wanting him to laugh too. But he only looked dazed and unhappy.

"Is Horn all right?" he asked.

"Horn's just tired." Wren was there suddenly with an armful of saguaro fruit. "It was too far for him to go in one night."

May and Pointer hurried out of the stream. Although May was hungry, she first helped Wren sit Evan down. Then she brought him something to eat. "If it was too far for Horn," she whispered into Evan's ear, "why wasn't it too far for Wren? Think how fast she must have traveled! To the stream and back again!"

Evan looked blearily at Wren. "She's strong," he admitted.

"She saved our lives," May said.

THAT NIGHT THEY SLEPT on top of a nearby hill. In the morning May insisted that everyone scrub their faces and wash their clothes. "We want to make a good impression on Horn's tribe," she chattered as she tried to comb Pointer's hair.

Horn, who still looked pale and sick, said nothing. They decided to start off immediately, following the stream's course. Again Horn took the lead. May could tell that the older boy was nervous. None of them knew what to expect from his people. They might accept a stray Sheep. But what would they do with a Coyote child—and three strangers who had no tribe?

It's possible, May realized, that we've come all this way just to be slaves again for new masters. That's what Horn is afraid of.

Ahead of her Evan shifted uncomfortably as they trudged up a steep slope. Wren had put mud on his sunburned back. "It itches," he complained to no one in particular.

Intent on her own thoughts, May swerved where Evan swerved. Automatically she watched the ground for cactus, snakes, and pointed rocks. Her mind turned on the ever-growing circle of questions.

What would the Sheep be like? Would they accept strangers into their tribe?

Who was Wren? Where was her tribe? Did she have any magic of her own?

Who was the fluteplayer? Why wouldn't the other children talk about him? Why had he disappeared from the cave?

May paused. Had she ever really seen the fluteplayer in the cave in this world? Hadn't she and Evan rushed out after that explosion? Had she first looked at the wall?

Preoccupied, May didn't notice the four Sheep at first, so she was irritated when Evan stopped suddenly. All the others had stopped too. Then May looked up.

A ring of tall figures stood on a rise above Horn's head. Their arms were muscled, their skin bronzed, their curly hair cut short. They wore cotton tunics with wicked knives fastened to leather belts. Like Horn, they had thick, heavy features. Like Horn, they were silent.

No one said a word. May began to wonder who would speak first.

"Hello," Horn mumbled at long last. He sounded painfully shy. Instead of stepping forward he stepped back closer to Wren. As he did so, his limp was noticeable. "I am Horn, son of Blue Tip and Red Horn. These are my friends."

May couldn't tell if it was natural for Sheep men not to show surprise or if for some reason they had expected five children to come marching into their village from the land of the Owls. At any rate, their expressions did not change. When it was clear that Horn had nothing more to say, one of the four Sheep gave a slow drop of his head.

"I am your uncle." The men did not meet Horn's eyes. "Come."

Without another word the Sheep turned and continued up the slope. They walked quickly as though to avoid contact. The conversation had lasted less than a minute.

"His uncle?" May whispered to Evan as they obediently followed. "This isn't much of a welcome for a long-lost Sheep!"

"No," Evan agreed. He lifted one eyebrow and looked worried.

The men climbed yet another hill onto a clearly

marked path. The children had to hurry to keep up.

"You'd think—" May began.

"Shh," Evan interrupted her. "Just be patient. This is a different tribe. These aren't Javelinas. I think they have more rules. They're more . . . formal. We don't want to offend them."

"Offend them?" May said loudly.

"Shh," Evan hissed again. "We've got to ask them about the fluteplayer, but we want to be careful this time. Please, May. Be quiet!"

TWELVE

After an hour's walk, they met the stream again. Here tasseled stalks of corn tangled with the green of trailing squash. The gardens were planted in the washes of the dry arroyos that fed the larger stream.

"They're catching the runoff rainwater," Evan told May.

May looked for signs of irrigation and found them in a small ditch that led merrily away from the river to a field of beans. The Sheep village, set back from the flood plain, was also impressive—much larger than the dirty Javelina camp.

"It's almost a town!" Evan said.

That's an exaggeration, May thought.

But the houses *were* built close together and set in a pattern of straight lines. Some of them had been made of rock, with thatched roofs and square entrances. As May walked past, she peered through the open doors and windows. In one building she saw women weaving on gigantic looms. In another a row of men were stripping the husks off corn. Like laborers in a factory, the tall Sheep worked steadily at their jobs, busy and efficient.

Busy, efficient—and strangely incurious.

For as the line of men and children passed through the center of the village, no one greeted them. No one called out or questioned them with a look. They might have been invisible, except that May saw one child stare and then run off with a guilty frown. She looked back at Evan, who only shook his head and mouthed "Shh!"

May did not feel truly concerned, however, until the Sheep men stopped before a small shelter of wood and stone. There they indicated that only the three boys—Horn, Pointer, and Evan—should enter.

"No, we stay together!" May protested.

Without moving a muscle, the Sheep managed to radiate disapproval. One of them, Horn's uncle, pointed to another hut close by. A Sheep woman came to lead the girls away. As tall as the men, with the same golden skin and short curly hair, the woman also wore a tunic and carried a knife. If anything, she looked even more stern.

May turned to Horn. But Horn's blue eyes were on Wren.

Slowly the girl let go of Pointer and straightened

her thin back. "It's all right," Wren said, nodding at May.

Together, Pointer and Evan followed the Sheep boy. He lifted a deerskin flap and disappeared inside. May and Wren hurried after the woman, who strode briskly into the nearby shelter.

At first the heat was unbearable!

It rose like wings to beat at May's face. It filled the sudden darkness with searing fog. A hand touched May's shoulder and pushed her to the ground, where embers gave out a red light, showing the stones heaped about the central fire. Gasping, May sat while more hands poured water on the hot rocks. Clouds of steam hissed up high and angry. May took a gulp and coughed at the shock of the burning mesquite-scented air. Already she could feel sweat run from her scalp, face, arms, and legs. She thought of Evan and his sunburned back! She hoped that the layers of mud would protect him.

As May grew accustomed to the light, she saw two other figures sitting cross-legged around the fire. Wren looked very small and vulnerable. The Sheep woman sat stiff and straight, her head high. Soon she began to murmur in the desert language. Her story ran together so swiftly that May could hardly follow it. More than anything it seemed a geology lesson: mountains rose, rivers dried, rocks turned to sand and soil. May began to feel sleepy. But when the woman put more water on the fire, the steam sounded like a thousand angry snakes—and May jerked awake. A seemingly endless river of sweat poured from her head, through her hair, down her arms.

She felt like an ice cream cone set on a Phoenix sidewalk in July. Help! she thought, and looked miserably at Wren.

Afterward, when they came out, the children were washed with buckets of cold water and given shifts of cotton and braided yucca sandals. May had never felt quite so wonderful, like a balloon, light and airy, about to float away. All the misery of the sweat lodge was worth this shiny, brand-new feeling.

"I think I could fly," she said to Evan. He grimaced, and she remembered his back.

Now that the five children were clean and newly clothed, the villagers could finally see them. One woman came forward to embrace the Sheep boy. When she finished, a man lifted Horn off his feet in a powerful hug. May guessed that these were Horn's parents. All the Sheep looked pleased and left their work to gather about the family. As though released from a spell, they talked among themselves and reached out to touch Horn's arm. No one said anything about his limp or the strangers he had brought. In their own way the Sheep people rejoiced.

As for Horn, he lowered his bright eyes and tried to hide his happiness. For the first time he looked as young as he was, not a man at all, but a smooth-faced boy barely sixteen.

With Evan and Wren, May stood a little to one side. "Isn't it wonderful?" she said to Wren. Then she shouted, "Hey!"

A Sheep looked at her in amazement.

"Hey!" May exclaimed more quietly at Pointer, who was slinking from a large building. In his arms he carried a bundle of corn.

"Pointer!" Evan whispered angrily.

"Pointer," Wren said with a sigh.

The three of them ran to catch the Coyote boy.

FOR THE NEXT TWO DAYS four of the ex-slaves rested in a hut and feasted on squash, corn, and freshly baked bread. Meanwhile, Horn fasted and went through more ceremonies. May and Evan decided to ask about the fluteplayer at the first good opportunity. Their chance came on the third evening, when the Sheep leaders called an official council. Unexpectedly, the children were invited.

Escorted by Horn's uncle, they entered a room made of gray rock. In the center was a circle of stone benches. These and the creosote torches on the wall were the room's only furniture. Slowly the benches filled up with heavy-featured Sheep men. Silently May, Evan, Wren, and Pointer followed Horn's uncle to their place. In a circle no one could be in the front or back, so May didn't know if they were important guests or casual visitors. She felt relieved when Horn came and sat beside Evan.

At first there was tribal business: when the corn

harvest would end, who was in charge of gathering the beans, which hut needed thatching. The Sheep men spoke softly, courteously, each in turn.

"This is interesting," Evan whispered to May. "In the Javelina camp the chief ruled mainly because he was the biggest. But this tribe seems to be more democratic. I wonder if they vote or if in some Sheep way they all just agree at the same time."

"Democratic?" May scoffed. "I don't see any women here."

"Shh," Wren said.

Horn's uncle was standing now. "We have been expecting you." The Sheep spoke directly to Horn. "The Owls told us that you were coming."

Beside May, Wren made a small noise.

"The Owls!" Horn repeated.

"No one crosses the land of the Owls without their knowledge." The Sheep's voice held a hint of amusement.

But Horn did not seem amused. "Since when do Sheep talk with Owls?" he asked.

Good question! May thought.

An older Sheep gave an approving nod. "It is not our custom," he agreed. "Nor do we like it. But these are strange times. Our magic is fading. There are days when we can no longer hear the seeds grow. Our eyes cannot see into the ground! The Owls tell us that it is the same with the Pumas. Meat is scarce, they say, and the Pumas cannot bring the animals to

them. Some Packrats have lost the ability to go without water. The Javelinas can no longer control the
rain. Even the magic of the Owls is weakening."

"We don't need Owls to tell us when something
is wrong in the desert," a Sheep declared harshly.

Another man spoke. "There is more, too. The
Owls talk of an even greater danger ahead."

At this, all the men seemed to shift in their seats.
"What danger?" Horn asked.

A Sheep coughed. "They will tell us soon, they
say. They have called a meeting. A meeting like this,
only . . . only with all the tribes. They will tell us
when we are all together."

May knew that for all the tribes to be together
was unusual. Still she was impressed by her friends'
reactions. Horn showed undisguised shock. Wren
paled to an odd-looking gray. Pointer's mouth hung
open.

"It has never been done before." Horn's uncle
spoke as though he understood how difficult this
meeting was to believe—as though he did not quite
believe it himself. "We are to go to the mountains
east of here, at the very edge of the Javelinas' land,
at the Needle's Eye."

"We do not know how this will help," the older
Sheep muttered. "But we are desperate."

The silence that fell now seemed permanent. Still
no one made a move to speak or leave. May glanced
at Evan. Should they ask about the fluteplayer?

Evan looked sick with indecision. May remembered what he had said before. The Sheep were more formal than the Javelinas. They had rules like an invisible net that hung in the air, a net of things that were proper to do and things that were not proper.

"Let's wait," Evan whispered at last.

Meanwhile, something else was happening in the council.

May didn't notice until she saw the expression on Horn's face. It had changed from general shock to a more personal fear.

The eyes of all the men, every Sheep in the room, had turned to Wren.

Slowly, the girl stood up. Her voice trembled when she spoke. "What about me? You say that you knew we were coming. Do the Sheep people also know who I am?"

The Sheep seemed to draw a single breath. Wren went on as though gathering her courage.

"Do the Sheep people know of these two here, who say they come from another world?"

Again Horn's uncle answered. "The Owls told us that the Javelinas would bring Horn and four other children to the meeting. Then, later, the Owls came and said you had escaped from the Javelinas and would come here instead. They said there would be a girl named Wren. They said that you were important."

The men waited.

May realized with a jolt that what the Sheep expected from them were not questions—but answers. They were waiting, Sheeplike, for an explanation.

They were waiting for Wren to tell them who she was.

May squirmed painfully on the stone bench.

The silence grew very loud.

THIRTEEN

A few days later May and Evan sat together in their assigned hut. As far as Evan was concerned, the Sheep council had been a complete failure.

They still didn't know who the humpbacked fluteplayer was.

They still didn't know how to get back home.

"Yesterday I drew a picture of the fluteplayer for the Sheep woman who brings us food," Evan confessed to May. "She looked completely blank. She looked like a blank wall! This morning I saw Horn's uncle. I tried again. He wouldn't say a word."

"At least he didn't push you down and bloody your nose, like the Javelinas," May reminded him.

"It's useless," Evan complained. "They won't even talk to us. Not about the fluteplayer, not about anything."

"You know," May said, changing the subject, "I

thought we'd be starting right off for the Needle's Eye. But no one seems to be in much of a hurry."

"Remember what Horn said," Evan replied listlessly.

Although Horn lived with his parents now, he came to visit his friends each morning on his way to the fields. The Sheep, he had told May and Evan, would not go anywhere until their harvest was over. Then the corn had to be ground into meal and prepared for winter. The Javelinas had to gather mesquite. The Packrats must travel from the south. The Pumas would be busy curing meat. The Owls and the Coyotes . . . well, Horn had said, and shrugged, no one knew what they did.

"I wonder what it will be like," May said now. "The gathering of tribes. Sheep and Coyote! Owl and Packrat! I can just hear Wren." She began to chant in the Javelina singsong. "The Owls eat sand. The Owls drink the blood of children."

"Let's go back to the land of the Owls!" Evan stood up suddenly. "I hate it here. The Sheep won't let us do anything. I'd rather be working like a slave. There's no place for us here. There's no place for *me* here. In this world, I mean! I always liked to hike and camp and be outside. But I want to go inside, too. I want to go where there are lights and air conditioning and TV and books and my family. My skin always hurts. I'm always afraid that my glasses are going to break. I hate it!"

May stood up too, dismayed by his outburst. Helplessly she looked down at herself. Her arms and legs were brown and hard and scratched in a dozen places. She could scarcely remember the girl she used to be—that soft, dissatisfied, slow-moving, angry sixth grader who had entered Evan's class in midyear.

Why, I'm more at home here than I've ever been anywhere else! May thought in amazement. I don't hate it at all. I like it.

Evan glared at her as though he could read her mind.

"Let's go to the Owls," he said insistently. "The cave with the fluteplayer was on their land, after all. Maybe the Owls will talk to us."

"Evan, the Owls are dangerous. And we're going to meet them soon enough at the gathering of tribes."

"Let's go back. I'll go alone if you won't go with me." Evan looked extremely stubborn.

"Hey," May said in what she hoped was a soothing voice. "Before we do anything, let's just go for a walk. Come on, Evan. We'll talk about this. We'll talk some more."

FORTUNATELY, that was the day they met Rhee.

She worked under a brush shelter near the edge of the Sheep village. Preoccupied with their discussion, Evan and May didn't see the rack of drying herbs until Evan had tripped over it. The brittle plants fell into the dirt with a thump. The tall Sheep working nearby held her hands still over a clay pot.

"I-I'm sorry!" Evan stammered as he gathered up the herbs. The woman nodded brusquely and returned to picking the leaves off a creosote branch.

May tugged at Evan to hurry on. But he only stared at the gray-green turpentine-smelling leaves. "Good for the stomach," he said softly.

May remembered his school report on the medicinal uses of desert plants. Suddenly she realized what the Sheep was.

The medicine woman stared at them. May knew that the Sheep had a strict division of labor. Only the women planted corn in the spring. Only the men built irrigation ditches. At council the men made certain tribal decisions. But the women controlled the dances, the births, and all the healing.

"Repeat that!" the medicine woman demanded. She stood six feet tall. Her crisp hair framed a wide face. Her pale blue eyes glinted like two pieces of early morning sky.

"The creosote. It's good for stomach cramps," Evan told her. "And you can warm the branches for rheumatism. If you chew it, you can put it on a snakebite."

He looked smug. May had a sudden memory of their sixth-grade science teacher, Mrs. Garcia, smiling warmly at the red-haired boy.

Then May glanced up at the Sheep woman's face. This woman was not smiling. Men were not sup-

posed to know such things. Thoughtfully the medicine woman stepped forward. Feeling foolish, May
and Evan stumbled back.

"Wait!" May said quickly. "Where we come
from, in our tribe, anyone can learn this. It's not just
for women."

The Sheep furrowed her brows at the mention of
"our tribe." Then her expression became the wall
that both May and Evan found so annoying. May
guessed that behind this wall there were bombs ex-
ploding and rockets in the air.

When the Sheep spoke, however, her voice was
calm.

"What else do you know?" she asked as she
stepped aside to let Evan see her collection of plants
on the ground. Some looked fresh as though just
picked. Others had dried to a sinister black.

This was the time to say "Nothing else" and
leave. May expected Evan to do just that. Instead he
pointed to a pile of mesquite branches.

"You can use the sap of the mesquite for sore
throats, and the leaves for skin sores and infections."

"For sores?" The woman brushed her hand over
the leaves as though stroking a cat. "How?"

Evan looked confused. It had just been a report
for school. He closed his eyes. "Not leaves," he said
at last. "Gum. You mash up the mesquite gum to a
paste and put that on boils and cuts."

"Mmm," the woman murmured, and pushed the

branches aside. She never mentioned the subject again.

But that afternoon she let May and Evan stay with her. When evening fell, she walked them back to their hut. There they basked in Wren's and Pointer's admiration. How had they gotten a Sheep to talk to them? And of all Sheep, Rhee—the head medicine woman!

Evan didn't mention going back to the land of the Owls. The next day they cautiously returned to the brush shelter. Within a week Rhee was letting them help in her work. Evan, of course, was more interested than May. But May came along with a sense of relief. Evan seemed happier now. And May was intrigued by Rhee herself. Horn said that the medicine woman was different from the other Sheep. She was too curious and too arrogant and too self-sufficient. Also, she worked alone, unlike the rest of the village. Her apprentice had died a year before, and she had not yet accepted a new one.

I guess not all the Sheep are alike, May thought. It's not *such* a boring tribe.

As they got to know Rhee better, they discovered something even more important. Rhee was the first person who did not try to stop them from talking about the fluteplayer. She never asked questions, and she never answered any. But at least she listened without putting on that blank-wall expression. Soon they had told her everything. How Evan had followed May up the hill and grabbed her wrist just as she touched the fluteplayer's hump. How they had heard music and the crash of cymbals. How the Javelinas had pushed Evan down for drawing the humpbacked fluteplayer in the sand. How, when they returned to the cave, the picture of the fluteplayer was gone.

"She's like my older brother," Evan told May later, "the one that plays the saxophone. She's open-minded. She really listens."

In the end Rhee did more than that. One night as they walked back to the hut, the Sheep woman put a hand on Evan's shoulder. She seemed very large to May—and very beautiful.

"I will tell you something," Rhee said, "and then don't ask me to say more. There is one person who can speak to you about the fluteplayer."

Evan and May stood still in the desert twilight. *Who are you? Who are you?* a quail called from far away.

"Who?" Evan asked in a husky voice.

Rhee smiled. "Ask your friend," the Sheep woman replied. "Ask Pointer, the Coyote boy."

FOURTEEN

That night, at long last, May and Evan found out more about the mysterious humpbacked fluteplayer.

When Evan confronted Pointer, the little boy promptly climbed into Wren's lap. From that safe position he stared at Evan like a fox staring balefully from the brush.

"You might as well tell us," Evan argued. "We already know that you know something." Evan used a tone that even Pointer recognized. This was a conversation that could not be turned aside, avoided, or made into a joke.

"Rhee told us to talk to you," May said. "And she's the head medicine woman."

Pointer squirmed.

"Look at it this way." Evan was relentless. "We're not going to stop asking you these questions. And you have to live with us!"

Now Wren spoke up unexpectedly. "The Sheep say that the desert is changing. Perhaps it is also time for us to change. It is time to give up your secrets, Pointer."

May eyed Wren. There had been an odd note in the girl's voice.

Pointer frowned.

Then he told them the truth.

As Evan had suspected, the fluteplayer was the key to everything—the source of all magic in the desert. All the tribes knew and worshiped him. But only the Coyote tribe could say his name. It was the Coyotes who carried with them the sacred skin on which the fluteplayer was drawn. It was the Coyote chief—a new one chosen every two years—who slept on the skin and dreamed the dreams of the fluteplayer.

"Don't blame him for not telling you before." Wren hugged Pointer. "Don't blame any of us. We couldn't talk to you about the fluteplayer. He is part of the Coyotes' magic. When we pray to him, we do it when the Coyotes come to trade. When he speaks to us, it is through the Coyotes. Rhee was very bold to say what she did."

"I've told you all I can." Pointer looked earnest. "Now you must wait for my mother. She is coming here to travel with the Sheep to the Needle's Eye."

"Yes," Wren said. "His mother was named Coyote chief just before the sacred skin was stolen by one of the Javelinas. Without the skin the Coyotes cannot dream of the fluteplayer. Without such dreams the tribe has no magic. Pointer's mother had no choice but to do what the Javelinas asked and trade away her son. Now she is coming to get him back."

"She would have come for me anyway," Pointer insisted, "when her time as chief was over."

"That's all we know," Wren said, ending the conversation. "Now you must wait for her. Wait for the Coyotes."

THIS TIME May and Evan did not have to wait long. The wild and wandering Coyotes came within a few days, sooner than anyone had expected. Loudly, gaily, dramatically, they danced into the Sheep village wearing turquoise earrings and the feathers of red cardinals and green parrots in their hair. While the rest of the Coyotes played instruments and sang, the chief grabbed Pointer and wrapped him in her arms. Like Pointer, she had a mischievous smile, sharp features, and straw-colored hair. Like the other Coyotes, the chief's skin was yellow and smooth, her eyes quick and not at all straightforward.

"Keep your eyes on Pointer's mother," Evan said as they followed the Coyotes back to their new camp, set suspiciously close to the Sheep's cornfields. By now a male Coyote was carrying Pointer on his shoulders. The little boy held tightly to the man.

"Is that his father?" May wondered.

"Pointer looks so happy." Wren's voice was sad. "He'll go live with his family now, just like Horn."

"Some of the Coyotes are playing flutes!" Evan exclaimed excitedly.

Not only flutes, May thought. This tribe has an entire orchestra.

All in all, the new Coyote camp was incredibly loud. The beating of drums, jangling of tambourines, piping of flutes, and strumming of guitars competed with the yells of children and chatter of adults. Occasionally the women threw back their heads and made trilling sounds that were piercingly high. These in particular sent a responsive shiver down May's spine. This was just one band, no more than thirty Coyotes. But they seemed to make the noise of a hundred.

Even as the three children watched and as the rest of the Coyotes continued to celebrate, the chief kissed her son and went off to speak to the Sheep's council.

In a very short time the news of what she told them spread.

The Owls' business had become urgent. The gathering of tribes was to be earlier than planned. The Pumas and Packrats were already on their way to the Needle's Eye. The Javelinas had been warned to hurry. The Sheep were expected to leave in a week.

The council had never known such confusion. The tribe still had to prepare food for winter storage, select those who would stay behind in the village, pack supplies, and hold a dance to bless the journey. They were not used to making so many decisions so fast. It was not Sheeplike.

"The desert is changing," Wren said again.

"Is that so bad?" May asked.

Wren didn't answer.

MEANWHILE, Evan held Pointer to the promise he'd made—to arrange a meeting with the Coyote chief. She agreed with a great show of generosity. Like a royal princess, she waited for them inside her luxurious tent. There, on a bed of rabbit furs, she sat surrounded by feathered ornaments, colored cloth, and musical instruments. Her flaxen hair fell loose about her face. Regally she nodded as May, Evan, and Wren came in.

Then, unlike any Sheep or Javelina, she went right to the point.

"I drew the fluteplayer," she admitted to the children. "I drew him in the cave in the land of the Owls."

"Why?" Evan exclaimed. "Why bring us here!"

"But I did not know *you* were coming." The chief smiled at him. "I only did what my dream told me to do—to go to the cave in the land of the Owls and draw the fluteplayer on the gray granite wall. Even as I made the lines, the marks of my charcoal stick disappeared. When I was done, it was as though I had never drawn anything at all. I knew that this was a great magic. I waited all that day for something more to happen. Then, finally, I left. What the fluteplayer did, afterward in your world, I have no way of knowing. It was his power, not mine, that brought you here."

Evan was silent. May thought furiously. Despite the Coyote chief's friendly manner, she wasn't being much help.

"Have you ever done this before?" May glanced at Wren. "Did you help bring Wren to this world when she was a baby?"

"No." The woman narrowed her eyes and contemplated Wren. Then she gave a shrug, as though to emphasize that none of this mattered to her in the least.

May remembered that this woman had traded away her own son. Maybe it wasn't so hard to understand after all. Wren had told them how important the sacred skin was to the Coyotes. Still, May thought, to let your only child become a slave to the Javelinas! It was a cold thing to do.

They could expect no sympathy here.

"We need to talk to the fluteplayer." Evan was using his most reasonable voice. "How can we do that?"

"Oh!" The woman laughed. "He is a god and you cannot talk to him. We know him through the dreams he sends us as we sleep on the sacred skin. The Coyote chief dreams, and if the fluteplayer has a message, the Coyotes bring it to the other tribes.

We trade and sing and talk of the fluteplayer. That is our magic."

"Well, they say that the tribes' magic is fading in the desert," May said bluntly. "Is yours fading too?"

At this the chief looked angry—and frightened as well. "That's no business of yours!" she snapped. "Tribeless children! Is this why you came to me?"

"No, no, no," Evan assured her. "We have nothing to do with what is happening in the desert. We're here by mistake."

There was something of a pause.

"By mistake?" the Coyote chief said with real surprise. "I don't think that the fluteplayer would make such a . . . mistake."

May felt more and more off balance. What purpose could she and Evan have in this world?

"We're here by mistake," Evan repeated irritably, "and now we want the fluteplayer to take us back! You must dream of him again and tell him that."

Now the Coyote looked as blank as any Sheep. She spread her hands palms up and said quite innocently, "Certainly! I will! But I cannot dream, you know, until the full moon. That is our tribal law. You must wait until then."

The next full moon was weeks away.

Evan's face seemed to crumple. Suddenly he looked very young. "I'm tired of waiting," he said forlornly. "I'm tired, I'm tired!" His voice began to rise.

May reached out and put a hand on his shoulder. "Evan, hold on," she said deliberately in English. "I'm here. We'll go home together. I'll help you find a way!"

The red-haired boy stared at her. His eyes were hard and angry. May hesitated before speaking again. Did she really mean this?

"Evan, I promise you," she said. "I promise that I'll help. We'll find a way back . . . together."

As she held his arm, May felt something deep in Evan's body relax. There was no explosion of cymbals and drums, no sound of a magic flute. But some tension in the air seemed to loosen. May breathed deeply. She had promised. She would do this for Evan.

Now I can't stay, she thought, even if I wanted to. We'll go back together.

Somehow they had both known this was necessary.

"Thank you," Evan said.

"Huh!" The Coyote chief watched them.

"On the next full moon," Evan said with dignity, "you'll dream us a message to the fluteplayer."

"The next full moon!" The Coyote chief stood up. Her teeth flashed in a brilliant smile even as she dismissed them. "Of course. Absolutely. On the next full moon!"

FIFTEEN

With that glib assurance, May and Evan had to be content.

At least they had no time to brood. The next evening was the big dance—the night before they were to leave for the Needle's Eye. May sat with Evan and Wren in a small group that included Horn, Pointer, and their families. Starting at dusk, a long line of Sheep men and Sheep women began to weave through a circle of fires laid in the center of the village. For an hour they spun a ribbon of movement that rippled to the soft tap of a drum.

Then as the soft tap-tap grew stronger, the two lines melted away into darkness. Now the tempo changed dramatically, and two male Sheep circled each other in the middle of the circle enclosed by flames. The two Sheep charged, leaping higher and higher, barely missing each other—until May felt sure that they must crash. The drum beat hard. The violence surprised May. When the two men faltered, another two took their place, and then another two. This time they were women.

Pound, pound, pound! Faster and higher the dancers leaped. Pound, pound, pound! May stamped her feet and cried out to the pulse of the drum. She echoed the rhythm with a fist on her knee.

The dance lasted all night. Off and on May dozed, only to wake again and feel her heart race at the sight of the Sheep, both male and female, charging and leaping in the fires' glow.

Then as thin lines of red threaded the sky, the Sheep men and women again began their slow weaving. The sun rose above the eastern hills.

Casually the Sheep drifted away.

May got stiffly to her feet. She had slept only a few hours that entire night. Still, she felt strangely clearheaded.

"It's a good day," she said, "to begin a journey!"

"To the Needle's Eye!" Evan, too, looked oddly refreshed.

"To the gathering of tribes!" Wren gave a rare laugh.

BY LATE MORNING the Sheep were well on their way. Half the tribe, including all the younger Sheep children, stayed behind in the village. The other half, hundreds of men and women, started east carrying heavy deerskin knapsacks. May, Evan, and Wren kept to the back of the marching line. Horn traveled with his family. Rhee brought up the rear. To the side a few men with knives roamed up and down the trail, on the lookout for game or signs of danger.

The Sheep, of course, had organized the journey with regular stops for rest and refreshment. Except for the scouts, everyone had a pack to lift, put down, and lift again. May knew that her own burden was light compared with the others. Still, her shoulders protested the extra weight. After last night's dance, she wanted to stride large and free through the beautiful desert. She wanted to move again to the beat of the drum!

As the day wore on, the lack of sleep made them all cranky. Dust kicked up by marching feet became a constant irritant. No one had much to say.

In the lead, Pointer and his band traveled happily in Coyote style, clothed only in loincloths, carrying few supplies, and stopping often to gather mesquite and paloverde beans. With their yellow skin and light hair, the Coyote tribe blended into the desert as easily as real coyotes.

"I wish we could walk with them," May said wistfully to Wren.

Later, when the Sheep rested for the night, the children learned that two more Coyote bands had joined the first.

"They're a small tribe," Horn explained. "They separate and travel the desert in groups of twenty or thirty, sometimes less."

Each night in the seven days it took to reach the

Needle's Eye, Horn came to share with them a meal of dried corn and squash. Sometimes Rhee came as well, and the two talked with a growing sense of amazement. Sheep and Coyote! Side by side! Of course, Coyotes had come before to trade and sing of the fluteplayer. But they were always few in number, and they had stayed only a few days. Never before had so many Coyotes and so many Sheep been together for so long.

"I'm learning some of their medicine," Rhee admitted one evening. "They mix the seed pod of the night-blooming cereus with deer grease. It makes a good ointment. Really, you know, Coyotes aren't so bad."

IN A MOUNTAIN RANGE rich with saguaro and barrel cactus, the Needle's Eye was a thin spire of granite rising high above the other peaks. At its base spread a small valley. Thousands could camp here— if they were willing to camp together.

As they entered the valley, Evan tugged at May's arm. "I've been here before with my family," he whispered. "I took a hike there, up that canyon, with my sisters. My parents came too. We stayed out all night."

"It wasn't here. This isn't our world, Evan," May reminded him a little harshly. "This place just looks the same."

No one was surprised to find the entire tribe of five hundred Owls already settled. The lordly Owls

had picked the highest ground for their campsite.
From this view they could look out over the other
tribes and assign each a place.

Dutifully the Sheep went where they were told.

The Coyotes did the same.

The Pumas came next and were put by the spring
that trickled at the mountain's base. By the Owls'
command, no one could camp right at the spring,
since they all needed to share its water. But the hot-
tempered Pumas had the privilege of being closest.

"The council fears the Pumas so near," Horn
said as they ate one evening.

"But everyone has promised to be peaceful."
Wren huddled next to May.

"What do Pumas know of peace?" Horn quoted
his uncle. "The women are more savage than the
men and they eat only meat to give them strength.
All the Pumas are warriors, and to become a warrior
in the Puma tribe you must kill the spotted jaguar
with your bare hands, without the help of magic."

"Barehanded?" May gave Evan a look of dis-
belief.

But the very next day she saw a Puma up close
and changed her mind. She was filling a gourd at the
spring. Suddenly, with one flick of her hand, a tall
woman pushed May aside to fill her own container.
This hand was impressive—long and heavily scarred.
The Puma's face was also impressive, with a large
nose and green eyes. On leaving, she stared hard at
May. Perhaps the Puma thought this odd-looking,

tribeless girl was no better than an animal because just then May felt a pressure inside her head. The woman was trying to control her thoughts! May pushed back with a burst of mental outrage. The Puma smiled and showed her teeth, filed into sharp points.

The next tribe to arrive were the small but graceful Packrats. They stood about four feet high, with smooth brown skin, bright brown eyes, and long black braids. All their clothing was made of coarse fiber, and their feet were bare.

"Horn says they don't eat meat and they don't garden. They live entirely from what they gather," Evan told May and Wren. "Their tribe is a real democracy, too, not like the Sheep. Every Packrat over thirteen, male and female, gets a vote. On the other hand," Evan went on with genuine interest, "the Pumas have no government or organization at all! It's strict anarchy in their camp."

"Fascinating." May walked up and down in front of the small cooking fire. "Wonderful. That *is* exciting. The Pumas only eat meat, and the Packrats don't eat at all. The Sheep are scared silly and hold a council every day. The Coyotes are busy stealing food or borrowing it. And the Owls won't say a word to anyone about anything."

Evan had listened to most of this before. "Horn says the Packrats have set up a game with dice and sticks," he murmured informatively. "They're compulsive gamblers."

"Let's go see." May stopped her pacing. "Let's visit the Packrats! I hate just staying here in camp!"

Wren put down the gourd she was waterproofing with creosote pitch. "No one is to visit another tribe without permission from the Owls."

"But why?" May complained. "I'm sure they don't mean we can't take a little walk."

When Evan only shrugged, May started out alone. She felt wonderfully adventurous. Then just outside the Sheep camp Horn's uncle caught her roughly and sent her back.

Still pitching her gourd when May returned, Wren only shook her head. "There'll be plenty of excitement soon enough," she warned.

"What excitement?" May asked.

But as happened more and more often, Wren made no reply.

May didn't like to press the girl. Lately Wren seemed unusually troubled. Her yellow eyes were dark and bruised looking. At night she tossed and turned. At mealtimes she often gave away half her food.

"What do you think is wrong with Wren?" Evan asked May in a private moment that evening. "Is it because Horn and Pointer have found their own families?"

"I bet she's upset about the Javelinas coming," May suggested. "She's still afraid of them."

But that apparently was not the problem.

The next morning they woke to see their former

masters straggling into the gathering place. And it was May—not Wren—who seemed the most bothered.

"Why are they so late?" May asked faintly. "This is part of their land, after all."

"Laziness," Wren said, sounding amused.

She's not scared of the Javelinas, May thought. But I am! What if they try to make us slaves again? What if they're still angry that we ran away?

"You will be pleased." Wren spoke with quiet authority. "Tonight will be the gathering of tribes."

"Will we be invited?" May asked.

"Oh, yes," Wren said firmly. "We'll be invited."

What does she know? May had to wonder.

SIXTEEN

It happened just as Wren predicted. With the Javelinas barely settled, the Owls called a meeting for late that afternoon. Each tribe was given a place in the half-circle surrounding the Owls' higher camp-site. In all, the tribes totaled more than two thousand men, women, and children. Each tribe carefully tried to sit as far apart from the others as it could.

May, Evan, and Wren moved with the Sheep to their assigned place, until an Owl came to take them to special seats on the hill. The woman who led them looked like the man May had seen long ago by the Salt River. This time, however, May was not so easily impressed. Owls were neither as tall as Sheep, nor as graceful as Packrats, nor as fierce as Pumas.

Still, May reminded herself, these soft, plump people had a strong magic. And they certainly knew how to act superior!

Even now this Owl pinched in her mouth as

though just being near the three children was distasteful. Her round yellow eyes stared off into the distance. Her brown hair was tied into a coil at each ear. Long feathered earrings hung to her shoulders. Her manner was aristocratic. She led them up the hill, but she did not look at them.

May rubbed her sweaty palms against her tunic. Their Owl guide was trying hard to act unconcerned. But May hadn't felt so tense since the night of their escape from the Javelina village.

It's not just me, May realized. Everyone feels the same way. The anxiety seemed to spread from person to person until it vibrated and filled the desert valley. If we're not careful, May thought a little wildly, this whole mountain could break in half! Anything could happen!

Evan nudged her as they passed the Javelina tribe. In the blur of faces a familiar one emerged. The scar-faced woman. She stared at them in surprise. She hadn't expected to see her old slaves here, escorted by an Owl.

Then they were in front of the half-circle, moving slowly past the tawny Pumas and the yellow Coyotes and the brown Packrats. Slowly they climbed to where the Owls waited. May saw that they had been paraded—purposefully led—past every tribe.

The Owl woman pointed to a place on the ground in full view of the waiting audience. Obediently the three children sat. Looking down, May marveled at the strange gathering. The tribes do not mix, Horn had said. But here they were, all six of them.

From the line of Owls a man stepped forward. His skin showed the mottling of old age. His round head looked bony and pathetic, surrounded by wisps of gray hair. His yellow eyes glittered. His nose curved and his lips were very thin.

May and Evan moved closer together.

The Owl's greeting to the tribes was formal and quick. He reminded them of the changes that had come to the desert in the last year. "The Sheep hunger and the Packrats thirst. The Javelinas do not control the rain. The Pumas do not hear the animals. The Owls no longer fly so far. The magic of the desert is fading! And the Coyotes cannot tell us why."

Not a rustle sounded in the waiting crowd. Two thousand pairs of eyes focused on the one man speaking. May was half afraid he would burst into flames, as a leaf will under the focus of glass.

The Owl must have had the same fear. He swung out his arm and directed their gaze to the far north.

"Perhaps our answer lies there," he screamed suddenly. "Perhaps our magic is leaving us because we have been careless, because we have allowed the desert to be invaded!"

The man's arm stretched out even farther.

"There, to the north," he cried, "are the lands we once thought empty and taboo. That is where the Enemy lives. *That is where the seventh tribe lives—they who have come here from outside the desert!*"

A shout rose now from every man, woman, and child in the six tribes. Those few still sitting leaped to their feet. Those on their feet waved their arms or shook fists and weapons. The mountain rocked. Frantic, wild, furious, the six tribes protested this information.

A seventh tribe? From outside the desert?

May felt electrified by the crowd's energy. She looked at her friends: each wore the same startled expression. The meeting seemed about to dissolve into chaos.

When the Owl spoke again, the people quieted to listen. "We have been watching them for many months," the leader said. "They have entered the borders of our land, and of the Sheep's, and as far south as the Javelinas'. For a long time we did not know their purpose. They came in a small band, and though we called this meeting, we were not alarmed. We did not know if this was part of our fading magic. In truth, we still do not know! We were prepared to wait and see. Then some weeks ago they returned much larger in number, much larger than we are at this moment! They have become an army!"

The Owl shrieked fiercely. "Soon they will be upon us. Strangers! Outsiders! They have come from outside the desert, and they will destroy us unless we destroy them first. Unless we learn to live together, to work together, to fight together!"

Again the tribes roared their confusion.

"Fight together?" Another voice, it seemed, had

the power to silence the crowd. It was the Coyote chief, Pointer's mother, who stood up as she challenged the Owl. "That is a great deal to ask! And I find it strange that you did not tell the Coyotes of this Enemy before. You say you have seen them. But where is your proof? What do they look like?"

At these words May's heart seemed to jerk out of her chest. She knew what was going to happen next. With horror she saw the round eyes of the Owl leader turn to her and Evan.

The Owl's gaze held her own for a moment. May felt like a mouse caught in a glare of light. Then the terrible yellow eyes shifted to Evan. And then the Owl sneered, dismissing them both.

His eyes came to rest, finally, on Wren. Like the Sheep in the Sheep council, he stared at the brown girl. He stared at her alone.

In the swaying crowd two ripples of movement— one among the Sheep and one among the Coyotes— burst up the hill. The two ripples became Horn and Pointer racing to stand next to Wren. All five children were together now. In the coldness of her fear May felt a glow of pride. Whatever happened to Wren would happen to them all.

The tribes' murmur became a thundering wave. Still the Owl could be heard. He pointed at Wren. "They look like her," he said. "The Enemy is already among us. *She* is the Enemy!"

A powerful cry rose from the people below. "Kill her!" someone yelled. Later May would wonder who had said that. A vengeful Javelina? A mild Sheep? A mischievous Coyote?

"Kill her!" Now the entire crowd was shouting it. "Kill her! Kill her! Kill her friends! Kill them all!"

The Owl leader smiled.

May shuddered as Evan reached for her hand.

Then Wren stepped forward.

Her words did not carry far. But the Owl leader heard her. And it was to the Owl leader alone that Wren spoke.

"I am not the Enemy," Wren said. "Or at least that is not all that I am. You say the Enemy looks like me. But are their eyes yellow? Like yours—and mine? And can the Enemy fly? Can they fly like the Owls?"

The leader drew back. "That is for my tribe alone," he hissed angrily. His wide eyes widened. A strange expression passed over his face. He moved as though to stop Wren.

But she had already raised her arms.

She had already turned into a great horned owl.

Standing beside May, Evan gasped and squeezed her hand tightly.

Silently, with a soft fringe of feathers that cushioned the noise, with glistening wings that spread wide, Wren lifted straight up into the air. Her wings flapped harder, and she began to fly over and around the six tribes, high above them in a great circle, hooting triumphantly as she flew in the dim and darkening light.

Of course! May thought. That's how Wren saved us that night. She flew to the stream and back again, with the gourd in her talons. Perhaps she *is* part Enemy. But she is also part Owl!

May turned to see the hurt on Horn's and Pointer's faces. Why hadn't Wren told them? Why hadn't she told her oldest friends?

May briefly met Evan's stunned eyes. He had never wanted to believe that the desert people had magic like this. He had never seen any himself. Now he couldn't deny its existence any longer.

May looked at the Owl leader.

He had aged ten years in the last ten seconds.

Relief—as powerful as her earlier fear—flooded through May's body, loosening her joints and making her knees feel weak. The Owl leader would not have them killed now. He would never allow that to happen to one of his own tribe.

Finally May turned to the hushed and confused crowd. Everyone watched the hooting bird as it swooped over them, around and around.

How much simpler for all of you, May thought, if she had just been the Enemy.

PART THREE

THE
ENEMY

SEVENTEEN

May dreamed she was flying.

She held up her arms and willed the blood in her veins to dance with magic. She willed the bones in her body to grow light, her skin to shrink and then blossom into a thousand feathers. As she lifted into the air, the muscles in her back pulled effortlessly to spread her wings. She sailed up, proud and strong and giddy with flight.

Her beak opened to taste the wind, and the owl part of her scanned the ground for small movements. Although her eyes saw only in shades of black and white, that was more than enough. The owl part of her dipped suddenly in the hope of a tasty mouse or rabbit. The owl part of her felt greedy and hungry and superior to everything that lay below.

The rest of her, the consciousness that was May, exulted. Higher she flew, pumping her wings for speed and turning to make a sweeping pass over the rolling desert vista, into the wonderful, living, insect-scented night. Flying felt as natural as breathing. This was what she was meant to do. This was the power she had often felt thrumming through her arms and legs and heart.

May hooted with happiness—and woke up.

She lay on the scratchy Sheep blanket they had given her for a bed on the hard ground in the rabbit-skin tent that she and Evan and Wren shared. Outside the tent the rest of the camp also woke to the pink light of dawn. Soon, May knew, the Owls would be moving about, preparing food and receiving visitors. The leaders of the other tribes would come to talk about their preparations to fight the Enemy. All day long, there would be complaints and arguments and discussions. Slowly, the six tribes were learning to live together.

When May opened her eyes fully, she saw that Wren was looking at her.

"I dreamed I was flying," May whispered so as not to wake Evan. "I turned into an owl! It was wonderful!"

"It *is* wonderful," Wren agreed.

"Tell me," May begged.

"Oh . . ." Wren looked shy. "I've only done it twice. The first time it happened I didn't believe it. You and Evan and Pointer were dying. Horn hadn't come back. And I didn't know what to do. I began to run, and then suddenly I was up in the air! It just happened. Later I didn't know if it was real or not."

"You knew," May said with certainty.

Wren sighed. Her yellow, almond-shaped eyes looked exotic in her heart-shaped face. "Yes," she admitted. "Flying over the desert that night, I knew that the land below me was *my* land, that I was an Owl. I knew. But I was also scared! I didn't want to tell anyone. I've always feared the Owls. Now I was one too! I am an Owl. But I am not completely that. I am also . . . something else. How could that have happened? It's horrible, May. The tribes do not mix. Yet I come from two different tribes."

May had rarely heard Wren talk for so long. From the corner of her eye she saw that Evan was awake. Like May, he didn't move or speak for fear of interrupting.

"I don't know what I would have done if it hadn't been for you and Evan," Wren was saying. "You gave me the courage to fly before the Owls— in front of all the tribes."

"We did?" May was surprised.

"You're different like me," Wren said slowly, thinking out loud. "You're different and alone in a strange world. But you don't seem to mind. You fight! Nothing is taboo for you, May. You're as brave as any Puma."

May felt embarrassed. She knew this wasn't true.

"And Evan," Wren went on. "He flies like an Owl in his mind. He's always trying to find out about things. Yesterday he told me that the Coyotes pick their leader through a contest. The best musician wins. I never knew that! Evan knows more about the tribes than I do, more than Horn or Pointer, perhaps more than anyone."

At this, Evan did move. "We're not anything special in our world," he murmured uncomfortably.

Wren only shrugged. She didn't believe him.

With a soft swoosh the flap of the rabbit-skin tent opened. An Owl woman had come with water and breakfast. She looked sternly at the three children as they got up and prepared to eat. By now May knew that arrogance was something the Owls learned when they were very young. They behaved that way even with each other. It didn't mean that much.

May sat down to the food with a deep sense of unhappiness. They would eat. They would drink. They would go outside briefly to relieve themselves.

Then as the sun moved east to west across the sky, they would sit inside this stupid tent all day long. They would sit where the air was stale and where they could not see the stars at night.

That fall, May felt more like a prisoner than she had ever felt with the Javelinas. At least as a slave, she had worked outside. Now while the six tribes prepared for war in the valley under the Needle's Eye, she and Evan and Wren were kept hidden in the rabbit-skin tent. Each evening May looked up to where the tent's central pole made an opening: here smoke escaped into the sky. During the daytime, she moped about and peered out the open flap. Sometimes she saw an Owl chipping spearpoints by the fire. Sometimes she saw a Puma or a Packrat hurry through the Owl camp.

When May could bear it no longer, she complained to Krakow, the Owl leader, even though he refused to talk to her directly. Because they had no tribe, May and Evan were nonpeople, almost nonexistent to the Owls.

"The Coyotes brought them to this world," Krakow once said to Wren. "They are the Coyotes' problem."

Now May faced Krakow, fuming when the round yellow eyes looked right through her. "But why can't we go outside?" she protested.

The Owl spoke to Wren as though Wren had asked the question. "It's too dangerous for the others to see you. You may be an Owl, but you are also an Enemy!" He spat out the words as though they tasted bad. "Your appearance would only cause trouble. The tribes do not trust you. And they do not trust your tribeless friends."

"Well, we don't trust you either," May grumbled.

Krakow pretended not to hear.

But Wren gave her a surprisingly angry look.

"How can you like that man?" May asked after the Owl was gone. "He put us up on show! We were meant to be sacrifices!"

Wren nodded reluctantly. Although Krakow denied this, the children knew that the Owl had

planned for the tribes to kill the Enemy and her com-
panions. In this way Krakow had hoped the desert
people would rally for war.

"But he protects us now," Wren pointed out.
"The Owls feed us and give us water. No one can
harm us. Horn and Pointer are even allowed to
visit."

"Thank goodness for that!" May said, and went
back to staring out the open flap. "If it wasn't for
them, we wouldn't know *anything*."

It was Horn who told them that the Javelinas
were teaching the Packrats to throw spears, that the
Packrats had shown the Coyotes a new food plant,
and that the Coyotes were helping Rhee gather medi-
cal supplies. The tribes were successfully working together.

Still, it wasn't always amicable. Pointer described
how a group of Pumas had disrupted a Sheep dance.
Pointer's own mother nursed a grudge against the
Javelinas. And almost every day someone was seri-
ously hurt in training.

Recently Horn had said that the tribes were sending for all the desert people who could fight. Only
the very old and the very young would remain at
home, where they would go into hiding. The war
with the Enemy was coming soon.

In the meantime May and Evan and Wren stayed
inside the tent. Evan taught May and Wren to play
checkers with small stones he had gathered. May
grew to hate the game. Krakow came to visit Wren

almost every day. And May, despite her grumbling, understood very well why Wren defended the Owl leader.

He was, after all, teaching Wren magic.

IT BEGAN WITH SIMPLE THINGS. May and Evan sat in the darkest corners of the tent while the Owl talked to Wren about how to fly in a storm, how to rise above the air currents, how to maneuver suddenly. He warned the girl that if she ate or drank while she was an owl, she would feel sick afterward. He spoke of the urges she might have to grab a young rabbit or even to find a mate.

One evening Krakow started a very different kind of lesson.

"You claim to be an Owl," he said. "And we have seen you fly. Yet you are also an Enemy. What else can you do?"

Wren stared at him, puzzled. May knew what Krakow was asking. The tribes did not know if the Enemy had any magic. But if they did, could Wren have inherited that power too?

Wren's face showed suddenly that she realized this as well. Now she looked frightened. A second power would be another wedge between her and the desert people.

"I don't know," she muttered. "I've never tried to do anything else."

Krakow blinked at her with scornful eyes. "Try now," he said. "We need to know."

Wren stared into the coals of the dying fire. As the nights became colder, she and the other children were allowed to burn a few sticks of mesquite wood. Throughout the valley the six tribes also had fires now and dressed in their heavier clothes. The Pumas rubbed animal grease onto their skin. The Packrats used a plant oil to hold in the day's warmth.

Next to Evan, May felt a prickling excitement. What else could Wren do? What else could happen in this strange world?

May also felt another emotion, something distantly familiar. It took a moment for her to recognize what it was. She was jealous! She was jealous of Wren in the same way that she had been jealous of Evan in Phoenix. Wren was magical. Wren could fly. Wren was the center of attention.

Stop it! May ordered herself. This is too important.

"I remember," Wren said softly, "washing yucca leaves for the Javelinas by the river. May told me then that I did exist, that I had to come from *some* tribe! Something opened inside me. I think that even then I could have flown like an Owl. But I did not dare."

Wren looked directly at May.

"Yes!" May whispered. "Go on, try."

Krakow waited.

Wren stared deep into the fire. She concentrated on one of its dying coals. "Grow," she commanded. "Leap!"

The coal burst into a flame that brightly lit the walls of the tent.

"Wow," Evan whispered.

"Fire," Wren said. "I can control fire."

By the time the flame had died, Krakow's expression had shifted from shock to anger. He got up abruptly. Before he left, he turned and spoke in so bitter a voice that May felt newly afraid for her life.

"We can be grateful for one thing." He seemed to hurl his words at Wren. "Fire will not help the Enemy in the desert! As for you," he said, pausing, "tell no one of this."

When Krakow returned on other visits, Wren progressed from lighting coals to flaming dry sticks and grass. This clearly took more effort. Once Krakow set a basket of water before her, a Javelina basket woven tightly with white willow and black devil's claw. "The water," Krakow ordered. But Wren could not. "Again," Krakow said the next day, and she succeeded only in ruining the pretty black and white container. Wren looked ashamed.

But Krakow was pleased. "At least we know you have *some* limits," he said. "You can't control water."

"Too bad," Evan whispered to May. "A basket like that, waterproofed and all, can take weeks to make."

Finally one day Krakow's expression was even haughtier than usual. He held his plump body very straight. His wispy hair had been combed. His feathered earrings looked new. He told Wren that the Enemy was now deep into the desert, in the land of the Pumas. The tribal leaders had decided to meet the invaders rather than let them advance farther.

"Stay with the Owls as we march," Krakow warned Wren. "Tell your friends to do the same."

"How many of the Enemy are there?" May asked.

This time the leader did not bother to ignore her. His face broke into lines of despair. His round yellow eyes darkened to mustard.

"How many?" the Owl whispered. "They are like ants in a hill—too many to count."

EIGHTEEN

May couldn't help herself. She was happy to be outside and marching—even to war! Gratefully she lifted her face to the sun and rubbed scented creosote leaves into her fingers. As Krakow had commanded, she, Wren, and Evan walked with the Owls and were rarely seen by the other tribes. This included Horn and Pointer.

"They visit us less and less," Wren complained to May. "They are always too busy."

"You miss them," May said after a long pause.

"They were my family," Wren answered.

May hugged the girl. It was easy to forget that Wren was only ten years old. She was two years younger than May, even if she *was* as tall, even if she could fly and make fire.

Together they wove a path through the desert shrubs and cactus. As they walked, Evan picked plants to give to Rhee. May chattered and tried to distract Wren. Their past was a shared bond. Soon May began retelling the story of their escape from the Javelina village, and this became their favorite subject. Looking back on it, they could laugh. How dramatically Evan had shrieked "She'll die! She'll die!" as he hauled Wren about like a bundle of sticks. How funny the guard had looked gagged and bound.

In unspoken agreement they did not talk about where they were going or why. Although she had once watched two Javelinas in a spear fight, May could not imagine hundreds of men and women trying to kill one another. The very thought made her feel sick.

Through the rolling desert the three children walked unburdened. None of them had been given packs or weapons to carry. At night the tribes continued to make their arrows, chipping stoneheads that they fastened with gum to twigs from the brittlebush. The leaders of the tribes seemed to be everywhere, especially Krakow, whom everyone accepted as head chief.

On the seventh day Krakow went up and down the line of marchers to warn them that the Enemy was very near. He made the warriors repeat what they were to do. He pointed to the nearby mountains and the narrow mouth of a box canyon where they were to rendezvous in victory or defeat.

"You must go there at the first sign of fighting," the Owl told Wren.

"I guess that includes us," May said loudly.

Evan shook his head at her. "There's no point in making Krakow mad," he whispered. "The Owls are on our side now."

That day, May and Evan and Wren walked silently in single file, not speaking or telling stories, but only waiting anxiously for something to happen.

It began when an Owl woman rushed over to Wren.

"Quickly! Go!" The Owl shoved the girl in the direction of the nearby mountain range. The three children started to run recklessly, dodging the sharp cactus. It was a hard climb up a steep, rocky hill. At last the woman told Wren to stop.

May and Evan were gasping like fish thrown onto a bank.

"You can go alone now." The Owl pointed to a dip in the mountains. "Go and wait! Don't stop. Don't look back."

The entrance was less than a mile away. May could see Pointer and the other children on this march also running to reach the box canyon. Rhee and some Packrats followed them.

"Hurry! Hurry!" The Owl turned as she said the words. The air around her body wavered, and she disappeared. In her place an angry bird rose up hooting.

"Come on!" Evan turned to go.

"Come on!" May cried.

"No," Wren said.

The thin brown girl stood completely still. Tears ran down her cheeks. It was the first time May had ever seen Wren cry.

"They look like me," Wren whispered, repeating Krakow's words at the gathering of tribes. "They look like me, only their eyes are not yellow but black obsidian."

"Wren," Evan exclaimed, "Krakow told us to go to the canyon!"

"You can't join the battle," May said suddenly.

"I've got to see it." Wren raised her arms. "I've got to see them. I've got to help somehow!"

Help who? May wondered. The Owls? Or the Enemy?

"No!" Evan shouted as Wren flapped her wings hard, her yellow eyes glittering. The great horned owl hovered for a moment. Then it was gone.

May took a step forward.

"Not you too," Evan said firmly, and he held her hand all the way to the hidden canyon.

ONCE THERE they discovered that a surprising amount of work needed to be done. The Packrats were in charge, and they had no objection to May and Evan helping. The children were told to gather as many stones as they could and pile them into a wall at the canyon's narrow entrance. If it became necessary, the desert people could hide behind that wall and defend the canyon against the Enemy.

May enjoyed working with the Packrats. They were natural builders, constructing their walls with incredible speed and placing the rocks just so. More than any other tribespeople—with the exception of Rhee, Horn, and Pointer—they treated May and Evan as equals. They looked May right in the eye. They nodded when she came up panting with a heavy stone. Sometimes her arms were so full that her sweat threatened to blind her, running down her forehead and into her eyes. Once she stumbled and almost fell. Then a male Packrat not much bigger than Evan came up from behind and patted her on the shoulder. It made her feel better.

All the while, of course, everyone was wondering about the battle. May worried over Wren the most. But she also thought of Horn and Horn's uncle and the Owl who had brought them food. She even thought of the scar-faced Javelina woman.

She and Evan carried stones for hours. At some point groups of wounded men and women began to stagger up the slope toward the canyon. Rhee set up a medicine tent and took in those who were badly hurt. The ones who could still stand and walk, however, only took a drink of water and then hurried to help with the stone walls.

From this May understood that the desert people were losing.

The retreat to the canyon went exactly as Krakow had planned. The Sheep were in charge of carrying the wounded. The Coyotes and Packrats crept in cunningly. The Pumas and Javelinas and Owls continued to fight until the very last moment.

Horn had come in early, staggering under the weight of his wounded uncle. The Sheep boy himself was bleeding from the head. Although Horn's foot dragged along the ground, his strength made him a warrior to be counted with the other men and women. Now he carried his burden to the medicine tent and then picked up a stone to take to the Packrats.

"Where's Wren?" he gasped as he passed May.

"I don't know," May almost sobbed. "She flew up as an owl. She wanted to help."

Finally, at an agreed-upon signal, the last of the fighters who were still on the battlefield ran for their lives. The Owls had no problem flying to safety. But as the Pumas and Javelinas rushed into the narrow mouth of the canyon, they were followed by a larger group of Enemy.

Then the archers behind the stone walls loosed their arrows, and the Enemy's triumph turned to dismay. The steep canyon sides prevented any further approach. The desert people turned as one to defend the entrance. The Enemy came no farther.

For the moment the six tribes were safe.

Wren was one of the last Owls to fly in. She tumbled to the ground and lay there in a tangle of brown arms and legs. May dropped her stone immediately and rushed to the girl. Pointer and Horn materialized from somewhere. Evan was away helping Rhee.

Quickly May checked Wren for signs of injury. Her friend's eyes looked strange—darkened to the color of mustard.

"Did you see them?" Wren whispered.

"See what?" May asked.

"Did *you* see them, Horn?"

Slowly the Sheep nodded.

"See *what*?" May demanded. "Wren, what have you been doing?"

"I couldn't fight," Wren said in a shocked, high-pitched voice. "I couldn't help. The Enemy looks like me! The other Owls were diving for their eyes, blinding them with their wings, but I couldn't. I just flew around and around. I saw it all. The people falling on the ground and not getting up. The Pumas, the Javelinas, the Coyotes, the Sheep, the Packrats! Falling and not getting up. Even the Owls fell from the sky. And I just watched."

"Wren, you sound funny. You look awful. I want you to see Rhee." May struggled to get the girl to her feet.

"Then I saw them," Wren continued. "Horn saw them too, didn't you? I saw the creatures that are with the Enemy. Their bodies are human. But the rest isn't! Their heads are the heads of birds. Their heads are huge, with feathers that flow down their backs! With big yellow beaks that open and shut,

cawing and cawing. They are monsters! Bird-men
and bird-women. At first I thought they were wearing masks. But they aren't. They aren't masks."

May looked at Horn. He nodded again.

"We all saw them," he said in his most expressionless voice. "Come now. Let's take her to Rhee."

AN HOUR LATER the desert leaders stood near the
medicine tent talking angrily. May and Evan hovered
over Wren, who lay curled on the ground. Rhee had
said that nothing was wrong with the girl—she was
just exhausted mentally and physically.

"We're trapped here to starve," a Javelina said.

"Or die of thirst," a Puma snarled.

But now Krakow the Owl revealed his cleverness.
Earlier, his flying scouts had explored this canyon.
At its base trickled a seep of spring water: the tribes
would not go thirsty. More important, near the
spring was another way out of the box canyon. It
was a hard climb, but not impossible. The wounded
and the children would have to be carried and, in
some places, lifted by rope. Also, their escape must
be accomplished that very night in case the Enemy
sent out their own scouts. Meanwhile, the strongest
of the Owls would defend the entrance. At the last
possible moment, when the Enemy realized that the
tribes were gone, the Owls could fly away.

The desert leaders looked doubtful. Many of
their people were hurt. Almost everyone needed to
rest.

May stifled a groan. They were expected to do something that very night? She looked down at Wren.

"This is your best plan?" a Puma purred at Krakow a little too sweetly.

"This," said the aged leader, "is my only plan."

So it was done.

The Sheep, who were the best climbers, acted as guides. The Packrats and Coyotes went up easily. The stocky Javelinas had to squeeze through the tight chimneys of rock. The Pumas turned out to be as good at nursing as they were at fighting, handling the wounded with extreme gentleness—and, May suspected, with a touch of hypnotic suggestion.

By sunrise everyone who had survived the battle had scaled the ridge and were descending the mountain on its other side. All that day the tribes traveled without a break. Some of the more badly injured had to be left behind in a hidden cave. A handful of Pumas stayed with them. Often May caught Wren staring wearily at the sky, watching for Krakow and the other Owls to return. May didn't know what the Owl leader had said to Wren about disobeying his orders. Whatever it was, Wren didn't disobey them again. She stayed with May and Evan.

Late that evening the desert people finally rested on the bank of a small stream. There Krakow appeared with a hard brake of his powerful wings. The other Owls landed close by.

A man once again, the Owl leader prepared to give yet another speech. This time, the crowd was much different from the one that had gathered weeks ago at the Needle's Eye. Looking about, May guessed that the Pumas, Javelinas, Packrats, and Sheep had each lost almost half their number. The flying Owls and clever Coyotes had done somewhat better. Still, nearly every member of every tribe had someone to grieve for. In the background, low and soft, Coyote flutes began to mourn the dead.

With one gesture Krakow silenced even that.

"Never again," he announced, "will we meet with the Enemy on an open battlefield. They are too many. We cannot fight them alone."

"No?" scoffed a Packrat made bold with pain. "Who will help us, then?"

"Have you more clever plans?" the Coyote chief snapped. "Something else we don't know about?"

"Yes!" Krakow the Owl said in his usual superior tone.

May had to admire the man. He wouldn't let them give up.

"Something you *do* know about," the Owl said. "Something we all know very well. Think. The Enemy comes from outside the desert. Do they know its food? Do they know the sand root or agave's heart? Do they know its secret places of water?

"Who will help us now?" Krakow asked the question and gave the answer. "The desert. The desert will help us."

The six tribes were silent. Then a few spoke haltingly.

"Yes, they have to find water."

"They'll send out parties. We can intercept those."

"I know of another box canyon. If we can lure them there . . ."

A Packrat approved, but said, "It'll be slow."

A Sheep protested. "It means wandering through the desert, never settling in one place, chasing and being chased."

"A strange way to fight," a Puma growled.

"The *only* way for now," Krakow said. "We are agreed, then? We will wait for the desert to do its work? We will stay together until the Enemy is defeated?" With his round yellow eyes Krakow searched out Wren, May, and Evan.

The tribes muttered.

"Together," Pointer's mother said, raising her voice, invoking her role as messenger and dreamer on the sacred skin. "Until the Enemy is defeated. Until the humpbacked fluteplayer sends us home. Until our magic is strong again."

NINETEEN

The winter months began. Krakow insisted that Wren and her friends set up their tent after every move and stay in there as much as possible. Sometimes the desert people went ahead of the Enemy to poison a spring. Sometimes the Pumas ambushed Enemy scouts as they searched for food. The Owls flew out regularly to spy.

The tribes were particularly interested in the bird monsters that Wren and Horn had seen on the battlefield. More than a dozen of these creatures lived with the Enemy, their fires set in the middle of the camp. With their great bird heads set atop human bodies, the figures could not talk and did not seem to have any magic.

To Wren the bird people were especially terrifying. At night she dreamed of their small glittering black eyes. May often woke to hear the girl talking in her sleep. "It's like magic gone bad!" Wren would whisper. "Like turning into an owl but being caught in the middle of it! Part bird and part human!"

Once when a nightmare got too loud and too painful, May went over to wake Wren gently. There in the darkness Wren confessed, "I don't want you and Evan to find the fluteplayer! I don't want him to take you back to this place called Phoenix."

"I know," May said. She looked over at Evan. His eyes glinted. He was listening.

The truth is, May thought, there's less and less chance that we *will* ever get back. Our only link to Phoenix is the fluteplayer. And our only link to the fluteplayer is the Coyote chief. Unfortunately, she's not much help.

Every full moon Pointer's mother promised again to dream of the mysterious humpbacked fluteplayer. Every full moon she had a new excuse for not keeping her promise.

May wondered if the Coyotes hadn't simply lost their power to dream. Everyone else's magic was fading. Perhaps the Coyote chief *couldn't* reach the fluteplayer.

May didn't tell her suspicions to Evan. She knew that he lived on hope. He counted the days as the moon waxed into fullness, and he suffered as it waned again to nothing. His bouts of homesickness were as strong as ever. He refused to resign himself to desert life.

*   *   *

As the war dragged on, Krakow continued to
visit Wren. He no longer taught her magic. Now he
came only to talk. This seemed odd to May. Still she
was glad for the information.

"The Enemy is in Sheep territory," the Owl
leader said one night.

"Do you think they'll leave soon?" As Wren
spoke, she stirred the fire with her magic.

"They are more determined than I thought,"
Krakow answered. "They must be hungry and
thirsty. Surely they weaken. But how much? And
what do they *want*? Treasure? Slaves?"

Abruptly Wren let the fire die.

May saw a shadowy Puma crouching to peer
through the open flap. "Your scout has returned,"
the man said. "The Enemy is marching for the Sheep
village that is nearest your own land."

Horn's village! May knew this was bad news.
Hunger was one of the desert's weapons, and the Enemy was growing very hungry indeed. When the
Sheep had deserted Horn's village, they left behind
all the food they could not carry: rooms of jerky,
pots of cornmeal, baskets of dried squash. Food and
shelter. Just what the Enemy needed.

Krakow shut his yellow eyes. "How is the
scout?" he asked only. The Owls who could fly out
and report the Enemy's movements were becoming
fewer and weaker every day. When they did come
back from flying, they were often so tired as to be
near death.

"Not good," the Puma replied. "The other leaders are waiting for you. They have called a meeting."

"Krakow." Wren spoke just as the Owl prepared to leave. "You will have to let me go this time. I can fly to the Sheep village. I can destroy the food at least."

Both May and Evan moved closer to Wren. Sometimes it seemed that their friend was changing a bit too fast. She was becoming too brave for her own good.

Krakow stared at the girl who was part Owl and part Enemy. He did not look grateful for her offer of help. Instead he looked bitterly envious.

In the end, of course, Wren was right. Krakow had to let her go—to burn Horn's village and all the food stored there. No other Owl was fresh enough or strong enough. Also, Wren could magic fire. By now, the six tribes knew that this was the Enemy's power. But Krakow had not yet revealed that Wren shared this ability. After her trip to Horn's village, everyone would know.

Once again Wren raised her arms and flew into the sky. Swift and sure, the wild bird soared over the vast glorious pastel-colored desert. May watched and ached to raise her own arms as well.

Wren returned from burning the Sheep village two days later, and all the tribes gathered to meet her. When she announced her success, there were smiles and even a few cheers from the desert people.

She's proven herself at last, May thought. They

accept her as an Owl now. Maybe they'll begin to trust us all.

Happily, that seemed to be the case. Wren began to walk around the camp during the day. Boldly, Evan went to Rhee and asked if he could help with the sick and injured. May spent her afternoons out in the desert again, gathering plants with the Packrats.

Still, May thought, the cost had been high. As though threatened by Wren's success, Krakow regarded the girl with increasing suspicion. Wren herself looked guilty and terribly sad. She mourned the loss of Horn's village.

"I destroyed it in a day," she told May. "Years of work. Rooms of food. Cornmeal. Jerky. Flour. Tepary beans. Rooms of cloth and baskets and tools!"

"They'll build it again," May assured her.

"The fire blazed in the sky!" Wren said. "I couldn't control it! I destroyed everything."

WINTER TURNED TO SPRING, and the tribes followed the Enemy to their new camp by the stream and smoking remains of the Sheep village. The Javelina chief died of a wound. Pointer's mother still did not dream of the fluteplayer. And the desert tribes came closest to despair.

Then one bright afternoon an Owl reported that some of the Enemy lay sprawled about in camp. A sickness had fallen over the army. The Sheep nodded—this had happened to them before, although never so bad.

As the desert people watched from a distance, more Enemy caught the disease and died.

"The Pumas think now is the time to attack," Evan said to May and Wren as they ate supper.

"What does Krakow say?" May asked Wren.

"He disagrees. He doesn't want another big battle."

May knew that the Owl leader would be under pressure to change his mind. Every day the leaders argued over what to do.

Before any decision could be made, however, an important new figure appeared in camp. The Pack-rats said that he had surrendered to them. He had wanted to be captured!

Quickly Krakow put the man in a tent set far apart from the main camp. Around this shelter the Owl leader put his most trusted Sheep guards.

Wren, May, and Evan saw very little of Krakow now, for he no longer visited Wren. Instead he spent his days in another tent talking to another Enemy.

TWENTY

The next full moon rose like a big round eye in the sky. Late in the evening May and Evan went to see the Coyote chief. Unlike Wren, the chief no longer had her own tent, but slept outside under the desert stars. That night May and Evan found her in a pensive mood, sitting quietly by a small campfire. May was not surprised to see Rhee there too. The Coyote and the Sheep had become friends.

It's an odd combination, May thought. But it was no odder than the other friendships that had sprung up between the tribes. Sheep and Puma children played hoopball together. Owls sought out Packrats. Even Horn and the scar-faced Javelina woman talked easily now. Why not? They had fought together against a common enemy.

Without waiting to be invited, Evan sat down and warmed his hands by the fire. His patience with the Coyote chief had long since ended.

"It's the full moon," he began bluntly. "Are you planning to talk to the fluteplayer tonight?"

In the firelight the Coyote woman looked tired. All the tribal leaders had spent many late hours with Krakow and the new Enemy prisoner. Still, Evan's question seemed to wake her up.

"I don't talk to the fluteplayer," she reminded him. "He comes to me in my dreams."

"Well, tonight is the night you are to dream of him again," Evan persisted stubbornly. "Remember your promise."

"Oh, yes." The woman's teeth glinted as she smiled. She chuckled with a hint of reviving spirits. "I do remember my promise. And I will do the best I can. But I am rather distracted this evening, you know. We have important news. It is not good to dream when there has been important news."

"No more excuses!" Evan exploded.

May noticed that his anger didn't have much force. He had expected this, after all. He was used to the Coyote's tricks.

"What *is* the news?" May asked with interest.

"A truce," Rhee answered. "We are talking to the Enemy about an end to the war. A way for all of us to go home."

A truce! What did a truce mean for her and Evan and Wren? May wondered in the sudden quiet. Where would *they* live? With the Owls? With the Javelinas?

"Home," Evan broke the silence bitterly. "I'm

glad for you, Rhee. I'm glad that *you* will be able to go home."

At this, even the Coyote chief had the grace to look uncomfortable.

As SHE PREDICTED, Pointer's mother did not dream of the fluteplayer that night. By the next day the news of the truce had spread throughout the camp. The word "home" was in everyone's conversation. All the desert people were tired of fighting—they were hungry and they were worried. In a week it would be the month of the painful moon. A large group like theirs would find that month very painful indeed! Even if they survived, summer would soon be upon them. If the tribes could not plant, gather, grind, winnow, and store over the summer months, what would they do when winter came?

Everyone agreed that the war had to end soon.

It seemed that the Enemy felt the same way. Perhaps the sickness had convinced them. Or perhaps they too had seeds to sow and food to gather. Whatever the reason, they stayed by the river and made no attack while Krakow talked with the Enemy prisoner.

One day the flap of the prisoner's tent hung open, and the guards were gone. Horn came to tell Wren that the Enemy had returned to his own people. This time he was accompanied by an Owl, a Puma, and a Packrat.

Three more days passed. Then a new rumor excited the desert tribes. Evan heard it first and hurried to May.

"The Enemy prisoner is back." Evan's long red hair, braided like a Javelina's, swayed in the spring breeze. "And another Enemy is with him! A bird creature!"

May and Wren were repairing their yucca sandals. May looked quickly at Wren. The girl's face was hidden, but May knew that Wren was afraid. Wren still dreamed almost every night of the monsters who were half human and half bird.

May herself thought nothing more about the two Enemies in camp until later that day, when Krakow appeared at their tent. The Owl did not sit down. He stood blinking at them, his feathered earrings bobbing at his shoulders.

Sitting next to May, Horn tensed. Horn had come soon after he heard Evan's news and had stayed near Wren all afternoon. Only now did May stop to think how strange that was.

"It's time you met the other half of your people," Krakow said to Wren. "Come with me."

In a rare gesture, Horn took Wren's arm and held it so tightly that her brown skin paled. "Don't go," he said urgently. "It's a trap."

Krakow's yellow eyes focused on the Sheep boy, and for a moment Horn seemed to stop breathing. Still he held Wren's arm.

May felt Horn's anxiety. She wished that Evan were here! "Horn's right," she whispered. "Don't go. It could be a trick."

The Owl ignored her. "Hurry!" he commanded. He sounded as deadly as on the day that he'd pointed to Wren and named her the Enemy. May had been afraid of him then. She felt afraid of him now.

Wren's own eyes began to darken. She touched Horn's hand. "It's all right," she said in a very careful voice. "I want to see my people. You can understand that. Let go, Horn."

She turned to May for help. Like any Sheep, Horn could be stubborn—as immovable as rock.

"I'll go with her," May said impulsively to the Sheep boy. "We can't stop Krakow from taking Wren to see the Enemy. But she won't be alone, Horn. I'll go too."

Sounding braver than she really felt, May challenged the Owl. "Why not? I'm tribeless. I'm nothing. Who cares what I do?"

Krakow looked at Horn. Then he shrugged. "Why not?" he said coldly.

THE AFTERNOON SUN, hotter each day, burned the back of May's neck. The wind threw sand into her face. Rocks jabbed at her feet. In silence she, Wren, and Krakow passed the last of the campfires and the six tribes. Then they were at the Enemy tent, where two Sheep kept watch. Krakow stood in front of the deerskin flap. He paused to let Wren go first. When she hesitated, he prodded her inside with an impatient hand. May crept in behind him.

Unwillingly she let out a cry!

A bird monster sat directly across from her on the dirt floor. Its head was larger than an adult human's head. Its yellow beak curved down like an eagle's. Its ruffled-looking feathers were glossy brown on top and dirty-white at the neck. Its shiny dark eyes darted to May's face. At her cry its head cocked to one side. The beak opened to reveal a thick gray tongue.

May realized then that the bird creature was also a woman, with a woman's body and a woman's full breasts.

Ahead of May, Krakow shoved Wren to the ground, then sat as well. The Owl waited a moment before speaking in a strange language. May could tell only that the words were words and that the speech was a pretty one, lilting up and down in a pleasant rhythm.

After a few moments, the other Enemy—not the bird-woman—replied. May turned her attention to him, and for the first time saw a reflection of Wren. There was Wren's smooth brown skin, her triangular face with its high cheekbones, her straight nose and mouth, her long arms and legs. Only the eyes were truly different, an almond of black instead of yellow.

Across from Wren the Enemy gave a sweet smile. He nodded and continued to speak in a tongue of soft *r*'s and long vowels. By the expression on his face and the chant of his words, May guessed that he was reciting a story from memory. As he sang, the bird-woman remained silent. Only her eyes seemed alive, darting about the tent as though searching for a way out.

For a long time in the heated afternoon the Enemy sang his song, again and again. The voice enveloped May in its lullaby lilt. The bird-woman, too, seemed to grow calm.

When the man stopped at last, without warning, May felt almost disappointed.

Krakow cleared his throat. "I don't fully know their language," he said. "But I have heard this story many, many times, and I am beginning to understand it. In truth, this is almost all I have heard in the last weeks. He has explained it in sign and drawing as well."

Krakow waited a moment. Wren was silent. The Owl went on.

"The Enemy, naturally, don't think of themselves as such. They call themselves the Deer people. And unlike us, they have always known that there were other tribes. For a long time they did not care to enter the desert. Where they live it is very cold for part of the year. The trees are tall, and the sky falls down in little white pieces."

Snow, May thought. She shifted nervously, feeling the black eyes of the bird-woman on her.

"Now," Krakow said, "according to their laws,

the chief of the Deer must be the son or daughter of a former chief. The position is inherited. A bird creature cannot inherit—although such creatures are born to normal parents. Throughout their history the Deer people have never reached the end of their hereditary line. That is, not until their last leader. This man was a good chief and much loved, but he had no living brothers or sisters or children of his own. He tried with many women, but none bore him a child. Finally he journeyed to the desert to find a female from one of the six tribes."

The Owl looked at Wren as though expecting her to finish the story. When she said nothing, he frowned.

"In the desert," Krakow continued, "the Deer chief found what he needed. We will never really know what happened, for the leader didn't return to his people. Twelve years ago he left them. And twelve years ago an Owl disappeared while out flying. We searched for her a long time and then mourned her as dead. She was, of course, your mother. I think that she must have died soon after your birth, and your father too. As you know, the Javelinas found you in a cave, starving and abandoned."

He paused to give Wren time to absorb this information. With its warm circle of bodies, the tent grew hotter and stuffier. Wren seemed poised for flight, unnaturally still. What was she thinking? May wondered.

Even Krakow looked concerned. "I don't know how the Deer people found out about you," he said sternly. "I think it has something to do with these bird creatures. They don't talk, and they don't have any magic we can see. But they must have some kind of power. Somehow they knew that you were here."

Seeing the Owl look at his companion, the male Deer spoke briefly. He pointed to Wren and then to the bird-woman.

"What?" Wren asked.

Krakow shook his head.

The Deer drew in the sand. First he outlined the figure of a man and from him drew two smaller figures—two children. One of the children had a large beaked head. The Deer chanted again, retelling part of the story.

"I was wrong," Krakow whispered. "The leader did have a child, but it was a bird creature and so could not be chief."

The Deer spoke.

"This one here"—Krakow hesitated—"sensed your presence in the desert. She is your . . . sister."

Sister! May stared. That was Wren's sister? *That* was her real family?

Now Wren was standing up. "What do they want?" she demanded in an unsteady voice.

"They want you." Krakow sounded very loud. "They want you to come with them. They have waited a long time. First someone else tried to be chief, and the tribe broke in two and warred with itself. When they grew tired of that, they thought of you. Of course, they would have been happy to conquer us as well." He permitted himself a smile, half-triumphant and half-sarcastic. "But they have changed their minds about that. The desert has defeated them."

"They're willing to leave, then?" Wren grasped at the hope.

Yes! May thought fervently. The Deer people were defeated now. They would go home. Everyone in the desert would go home.

"They *are* leaving," Krakow said, "and you are to go with them. They require that, at least."

This time it was Wren who cried out.

May jumped to her feet and reached for her friend so that they both could escape. But the bird-woman darted forward first, her beak twittering and her breath foul. She grabbed Wren's wrist just as Horn had done.

Wren tried to fight her off. She tried to raise her arms to fly away. But the hand held her firmly.

May smelled smoke. The edges of the deerskin flap began to smolder. Fire crept up the wall of the tent. Outside, a breeze fanned the flames and they leaped higher.

"Stop it!" Krakow's voice rose above the confusion.

"Wren!" May choked out. There was nothing now but black smoke all around her. There was nothing, suddenly, but blackness itself.

TWENTY-ONE

May woke in her own tent. Her throat felt sore and the skin on one of her legs hurt as though it had been sunburned.

"Are you thirsty?" Evan was there almost immediately.

May sat up and peered out the open flap. It was late morning. The sun was already high. Where had yesterday gone? What had happened? Where was Wren?

"Hey, hey," Evan said. "Everything's okay. You got some smoke inhalation. And your leg is a little burned. But Rhee says that you'll be fine. Wren will be fine too. She's still asleep. Everyone's fine."

That didn't seem likely. May remembered now. The Enemy was going to take Wren away to a strange cold land. The bird-woman was Wren's sister. Krakow had betrayed them after all.

May's head throbbed as she peered about the rabbit-skin tent. Wren lay still on her pallet of grass. She indeed looked as if she were sleeping. But May wondered and watched carefully. Suddenly Wren's eyes fluttered open. She shut them quickly with a rebellious frown. No, Wren wasn't sleeping. She was thinking. She was brooding.

Outside, Packrats and Pumas and Javelinas rushed about carrying supplies and dismantling the camp. Evan told May that the six tribes were preparing to move because a truce had finally been made. They would escort the Enemy back to the border between the desert and the northern lands.

At lunchtime Evan went off to find some food.

May crept closer to Wren's bed.

"Talk to me, Wren."

Wren frowned again. After a long pause, she whispered, "I'm sorry, May. I hurt you. I could have killed you."

May suppressed a shiver of fear. In all these past months nothing had frightened her more than being in that tent when it caught fire. Wren had done that! Without meaning to, in the violence of emotion, Wren's magic had reached out and set the world ablaze.

Magic is dangerous, May thought. It can't always be controlled. For a moment she wondered how she could ever have been jealous of Wren.

"That's right," May said. "You could have killed

me. And you did hurt my leg! So you owe me something now, Wren. You have to talk to me. You have
to tell me what you're thinking."

Wren shut her eyes, and May was afraid that she
had been too bold—too bossy, as usual.

But at long last Wren said, "I'm thinking of my
mother and father."

THAT AFTERNOON Wren talked. And May
argued.

"It's an ugly story," Wren insisted.

The Deer had come into the desert to kidnap a
female. Perhaps he had injured her so badly she
couldn't fly away. Then he had waited to see if she
could bear him a healthy child.

"How awful it must have been for my mother,"
Wren whispered. "Imprisoned by a man whose first
baby had the head of a bird! How she must have
hated me, the thing inside her!"

Later, when Wren was born . . . what happened? Did the man and woman both realize the
horror of it? Did the Owl woman kill the Deer and
then kill herself, leaving the infant to starve? Or did
the Deer kill her and flee into the desert?

"An ugly story!" Wren repeated.

Evan came in with some dried jerky. Wren refused to eat anything.

"But maybe that's not the story at all," May suggested.

Maybe the Owl woman *did* have an accident,

and the Deer found and cared for the injured woman. Against all rules, they grew to love each other.

"After all," May said to Wren, "didn't you grow to love Horn? And Pointer? The mixing of two tribes. Is it really that horrible?"

Perhaps love was why the woman did not return to her people, why the man did not force her to leave the desert. How, May asked, could a Deer keep an Owl captive for nine months? No, surely they had *wanted* to stay together. Afterward, when Wren was born . . . who knows what happened? There are many ways to die in the desert. Snake, falling rock, scorpion . . .

"Doesn't that make more sense than a woman abandoning her own baby?" May asked. "Or a father leaving the child he wanted so much?"

"Maybe it's a *good* story." May tried to catch Wren's eye.

But Wren would not look at her.

IT WAS NOT UNTIL early evening that Horn and Pointer found the time to come visit. They had been helping their families pack supplies all day. May was enraged by their callousness. Horn actually had a grin on his face! And Pointer danced about, full of jokes. They were in very good moods, considering what was about to happen to Wren.

They just don't care, May thought. Wren has to leave the desert. And maybe *we* do too, May realized suddenly. Maybe we are to go with her. We're going away forever, and they don't even care! They have their own tribes now. The tribes don't mix.

"Wren, if you don't want that jerky," Pointer said, hungrily eyeing the untouched food, "I'll eat it for you."

At this, May lost her temper.

When the tantrum was over, Horn and Pointer just stared.

"Well," Pointer said after a long moment, "it's not as if you are going away forever. It's only six months. And when Wren comes back, my mother has promised that I can go see her. I can visit the Owls!"

"Yes," Horn interrupted, looking self-important. "And if a Coyote can visit Owls, so can a Sheep."

"When I come back?" Wren said, bewildered.

They stared at one another.

"Didn't Krakow tell you?" Horn asked. "He made a big speech to the camp. Didn't he tell you?"

"Rhee told me about the truce," Evan said. "That's all any of us know. We haven't seen or heard from Krakow all day."

"I think," Wren said slowly, "that Krakow is angry at me now. I think not visiting me is a kind of punishment."

Horn and Pointer looked worried.

"What was Krakow supposed to tell her?" At least Evan had the sense to move the conversation forward.

"Yes!" May almost shouted. *"What are you talking about?"*

So for the first time May and Wren and Evan heard the details of the truce between the Deer and the six tribes.

Wren was to go with the Deer and live with them for half the year—and for half of every year to come. For the other half, she would return to the Owls. Krakow had warned the Enemy that if the agreement was not kept, he himself would bring Wren back to the desert. And the Deer would never see her again.

For both sides Wren could act as a hostage. Neither would attack while she was with the other tribe. On her part, she would have allegiance to the Deer, and to the desert, and keep each from warring with the other.

Wren puzzled over it. "I don't understand," she said. "Why don't the Owls just give me up to the Deer? Why do they want me back?"

"Don't you see?" Evan replied excitedly. "Don't you know how the Owls choose *their* leader? The Owls choose the most magical. That's you! All the Owls know it."

Wren sputtered: "Krakow is the leader. I can't be their leader."

"Sure you can," May broke in. "You've got the strongest magic, and according to their law, that's who the leader is. Everyone knows how the Sheep village burned. Everyone saw how far you can fly. You have the power of the Deer. And you can turn into an owl. You're the strongest Owl there is. Naturally they want you back."

"It's interesting," Evan mused, "what happens when the tribes do mix. They get stronger, not weaker. I mean, their children appear to have more power, not less."

Horn still looked worried. "Krakow fears you," he said to Wren. "He wants your strength for his tribe. But he also fears that strength."

"Oh, the Owls won't be happy," Evan agreed. "But they have rules, and according to those rules, you must return to lead the tribe."

"Queen!" May said unexpectedly. She looked at Evan. They both laughed.

"Queen Wren! Queen Wren!" May took Wren's hand affectionately. "You were the queen all along!"

TWENTY-TWO

Late that night, May sat up in her bed. She rose quietly and went outside the tent to where stars sprinkled the sky like flowers sprinkling the desert during a wet spring.

She saw Wren at the edge of their campsite. The girl's arms were half-raised. Her heart-shaped face was turned to the sky.

May could guess what Wren was thinking.

Wren could fly away now. She could escape to some corner of the Packrats' vast dry land. Alone, she could eat from the spiny trees and gather the greens of lamb's-quarter and dandelion. She could search for wild onion and sand root. It would not be a bad life. At least she would not have to live away from the desert. She would not have to tread a path between clever Krakow and the strange Deer. She would not live in fear of losing control—as she had done in the tent just yesterday. She would not have to claim a bird-woman as a sister.

May smelled the clean desert air. She remembered her own dream about sailing up as an owl. She remembered diving into the wonderful, living, insect-scented night. Flying had felt as natural as breathing. She could almost feel the wind tickling her feathers.

She thought of Wren's life with the Javelinas. The tribeless girl had been content. All the family she needed were Horn and Pointer. She had enough to eat and enough to drink. She knew what each day would bring.

Now everything was uncertain. The Javelinas looked the other way when they saw her. More disturbing, if Wren were to give an order, they would obey. If she were to tell the scar-faced woman to fetch a pot of water, the woman would fetch it.

Wren hated that.

May didn't really understand. She only knew that she wanted her friend to be happy again.

Well, go then, May thought. Fly away. Fly into the desert!

The summer night felt soft and warm. The mesquite trees sent out their sweet scent. A lizard rustled behind a rock.

Wren raised her arms higher.

What about the six tribes? May wondered. Will the truce be broken? Will the war continue? What about Evan and me? Will we go back to the Sheep? Or to the Javelinas?

Wren's arms faltered.

"Go on," May said firmly, "if that's what you want. If that's what you need to do."

May felt a movement behind her. It was Evan.

"Go on," Evan said.

Wren stood very straight. She knew they would not stop her. There would be no alarm.

Still her arms dropped. The moment had passed. She turned and walked back to them.

"How do you stand it?" she asked Evan. "How do you stand being so far from your home?"

"I don't know," the boy answered in a sleepy voice. "I really don't know."

They went back into the tent together.

There on the scratchy Sheep blanket May fell into a dream almost immediately. It was long and wonderful. It was full of amazing and interesting adventures, full of possibility, full of magic. In her dream May felt strong and secure and joyful.

This time, however, the dream was not about flying.

It was about Phoenix.

TWENTY-THREE

The six tribes and the Enemy traveled together for many days. On one particularly hot morning May finished her breakfast of burned cholla joints and then licked her fingers wistfully. It was the month of the painful moon.

"Remember those little green worms?" she said to Evan. "The ones that came out with the summer rains? I think I could eat one now."

With a sharp clap on May's back, Pointer attacked her suddenly from behind. "I have one right here!" He showed her his closed fist. "Open your mouth."

"Well," May hedged.

"Are you ready?" Pointer's mother stood next to her son. The Coyote chief was dressed in all her finery. Red feathers danced in her blond hair, necklaces looped the swell of her chest, copper bracelets jangled on her wiry arms.

"Ready?" echoed Evan.

May's heart beat fast. Wren came out of the tent. Now May could see Horn and Rhee walking toward them.

"You're going to draw the fluteplayer," Evan said quietly.

The woman smiled. "It will be my last act as the Coyote chief. My two years are nearly over, and soon another Coyote will take my place and dream on the sacred skin. For a long time I was afraid that something in the skin had died. I was afraid for us all! Then last night I had a dream from the fluteplayer. He has returned to us. I am going to draw him today."

May felt stunned.

The Coyote woman went on blithely. "Magic is returning to the desert people. The Coyotes will again be the messengers of the fluteplayer. The Sheep will grow fine crops. The Javelinas will bring down the summer rain. The desert will be wet and rich and green—as it has never been before.

"Come!" The woman jangled the bracelets on her arms. "Aren't you ready yet? We must go to the clearing of stones. It is a far walk."

"Wait," Wren protested weakly.

"Wait!" May echoed. "You had a dream last night? But there wasn't a full moon! There was hardly any moon at all!"

"Ah," the Coyote said, and shrugged. "I thought

you understood. I just said that so you wouldn't keep pestering me."

THE COYOTE WOMAN WENT FIRST, then Rhee, May, Evan, Wren, Pointer, and Horn. For a while it seemed that they were running more than walking. May wondered if this was to prevent further conversation.

Even so, between breaths, Evan managed a reproach. "You lied to us," he accused the Coyote chief.

"The dreams come when they come," she said serenely. "You can't hurry them. Listen, children from another world. In my dream last night I saw the six of you at the place of stones some miles from here. And I saw myself drawing the fluteplayer on a large white boulder. That is *all* I saw. All I can do is take you there now. It was the fluteplayer who brought you into our world, not me. If he chooses, it will be the fluteplayer who sends you back."

"But why?" May asked as she trotted behind Rhee. "Why did he bring us here?"

"Oh, it was all a mistake," the Coyote woman teased her.

"No," Evan said. "Even I don't believe that anymore."

"You want an explanation?" the chief said with a shrug. "I have none. We call the fluteplayer mischievous. We say that he likes to play—like a coyote pup plays, like the wind plays over the desert. Perhaps he has simply played with you. Or . . . perhaps not. Why did our magic fade? Why is it returning now? Perhaps we needed a reason to make us come together? Surely much has been accomplished. We have found a seventh tribe! The tribes are mixing. The girl Wren is in her rightful place. What part you had in all of this—I have no idea."

May turned back to look at Wren. Had they been sent to help Wren—half Owl, half Deer—find her way in the changing desert? Or had the flute-player simply been playing with them?

May would never know for sure.

I know that *I* have changed, she thought with certainty. I've changed as much as anyone.

"Gosh, we've been here a year." Evan had started on a new subject. "How are we going to explain any of this?"

May swerved expertly around a prickly pear. "We'll think of something," she said.

"We could always . . ." Evan murmured, then kept on thinking busily.

May was silent.

For another hour, and then two, and then three, they followed the Coyote chief. The desert seemed unusually vibrant and alive to May. She could feel its power subtly, thrumming through her arms and legs. Magic *was* returning to the fluteplayer's world.

Finally Pointer's mother stopped at an odd little clearing where a group of boulders rose in a tangled jumble. The woman did not give the children time to rest or talk. Instead she went immediately to a single slab of stone set slightly apart from the others. From a small leather pouch she got out a charcoal stick and began to sing.

"What does his hump carry?" she sang. "It carries the seeds of spring, the seeds of corn and squash, the seeds of the saguaro and the prickly pear. It carries babies, plump and perfect. It carries sandals for our feet and deerskin for our shirts. It carries obsidian, flint, and turquoise. It carries . . ."

The rest of them—Rhee, Horn, Pointer, Wren, May, and Evan—stood in the late morning light as the chief began to draw the dancing legs of the fluteplayer. As she had described before, the charcoal lines disappeared almost as she made them.

That takes some skill, May thought abstractedly. How can she remember what she has already done?

May watched as the chief drew the skinny arms and slender flute, the shoulder and big cheerful hump, the eyes radiating and round and mocking. Soon the drawing would be complete.

Why do I feel so numb? May wondered. Look at how excited Evan is! But it's . . . all too fast for me. It's happening too fast!

Horn bent close to Wren. May could hear his low grumble.

"Perhaps," the Sheep whispered, "you should say good-bye while there is time?"

Good-bye!

At this even Evan looked unhappy. May turned

to stare at each one of them. Horn. Pointer. Rhee. Wren.

Suddenly Wren was holding her tight. "No!" Wren cried. "We will *not* say good-bye, because you are not leaving. You must not leave me!"

"Wren," Evan said. "We have to go home."

Wren looked at him with blind eyes. Then she spoke only to May. "This is your home, May. Let Evan go if he must. But you can stay. Oh, May! I will be a queen, a ruler, a chief. And you can rule with me! You can be a queen too."

May held Wren just as tightly. For a moment it seemed easy. She didn't have to leave the wild desert. She didn't have to leave her friends. She could stay here.

"But Wren," May explained after the moment had passed. "You know I can't. I've promised Evan."

"You've got to let us go." Evan sounded surprisingly gentle.

"I can't," Wren said.

"Oh." May laughed through her tears. "You can. I know it. You can do this, too."

For one long second Wren hugged May. Then she stepped back. "I *won't* say good-bye," she insisted.

Just then Pointer gave a yelp that made even Horn the Sheep jump. The tall boulder began to glow with a silver light. The Coyote chief finished hurriedly.

May and Evan joined hands. Wren and the Coyote chief retreated so that two groups were formed: May and Evan directly before the drawing and the five others in a half-circle behind them.

"I won't say good-bye, because perhaps you'll come back!" Wren cried. "Try to come back! Try to come back!"

"Oh, yes!" May turned to look at her. "Yes. I hope so."

"Good-bye!" Evan said excitedly. "Say good-bye to all the Owls and Sheep and Pumas and Packrats and Coyotes! You can even say good-bye to the Javelinas. And to Krakow!" He slapped his hand to his head. "And Horn! Here, take my glasses! You can focus the sunlight to make fire with them!"

The boy threw his precious eyeglasses, and Horn reached up to catch them. As he did, an explosion seemed to rip the sky apart. There was the crash of cymbals and the beating of drums.

In one moment their friends were saying good-bye, and in the next they were gone. Wren and Horn and Pointer were gone.

In that same moment May once again heard the piping of the fluteplayer. The melody grew until it included everything: rock, stars, sky, light, saguaro, ocotillo, mesquite, paloverde, jackrabbit, scorpion, and snake.

It is the most beautiful sound in the world, May thought.

It was the sound of the desert.

EPILOGUE

TWENTY-FOUR

This time, when they found themselves in their own world, Evan was the first to recover.

"We're back!" he said triumphantly. His dusty, sunburned, scratched, freckled face looked utterly happy.

May looked around. Only the fluteplayer drawn on the rough boulder remained to show that her friends had ever existed. In many other ways this small canyon looked much like the fluteplayer's world, with the same weathered rocks, spiderlike ocotillo, and thorny prickly pear. May could not even see any houses or signs of human life. But when she breathed the air, she smelled something stale and metallic. When she stared at the horizon, she saw a faint line of pollution. And when she listened, she heard it—the frantic swish, swish, swish of cars on a nearby highway.

"Hey!" Without glasses, Evan's blue eyes looked

very young. He walked a few steps, picked up a piece of paper, and held it close to his face. "A candy bar wrapper!"

May had to smile at him in return. They were home. They were safe. And there *were* good things in this world.

Most important, she would be seeing her parents again! Suddenly the memories came flooding back. Her mother's face. Her father's jokes in the morning. She had missed them. Of *course* she had missed them.

"Come on!" Evan cried.

"Good-bye," May whispered to the fluteplayer even as she ran after her friend.

Already the red-haired boy was standing at a small rise of gravel and rock. "Look!" He pointed to the ribbon of asphalt below them. "I can't see too well, but I know we're not back in Papago Park. The fluteplayer's world matched the geography here, and I think I know what highway that is. We're east of Phoenix now, not far from the San Carlos Apache Indian Reservation. This highway leads to a town called Superior."

His voice trembled a little. May felt the same way.

"Let's go see," she said roughly.

"Let's go!" they said together, and galloped down the hill.

It was nearly noon, and the highway shimmered in wavy lines of heat.

May and Evan stood for a moment by the shoulder of the road. A blue sports car sped by. May jumped back in fear. Another car followed, and another and another. Evan opened his mouth, but May couldn't hear him over the roar of engines.

Just then a battered pickup pulled over to offer a ride. As the driver slowed down, May realized how strange they must appear—with their unwashed hair, yucca sandals, and coarse cotton tunics.

"What the—?" began the pretty Apache woman in the red truck.

"We're on a wilderness field trip," Evan said smoothly. "You know, a field trip for school that teaches wilderness skills, survival, that kind of stuff."

May looked at him admiringly. Obviously he had rehearsed this speech.

"We've just been out alone in the desert," Evan went on. "Only, uh, now we've got to get back to Phoenix. We've got to get back home."

The dark-haired woman seemed suspicious. "I'm only going as far as Superior," she warned. "And I'm full up here." She gestured at the infant sleeping in a car seat beside her. The floor of the truck was filled with packages and newspapers.

"That's fine, fine!" Evan nearly screamed. "We'll ride in back!"

He nudged at May to climb into the truck. She started to swing over and then paused. Although Evan might not believe it, she had also been thinking about their return to Phoenix. And she had a few ideas of her own. Now she approached the cab and stood on tiptoe to look into the driver's face. "Do you have today's newspaper?" she asked carefully.

"Today's paper?" The woman rummaged and handed her a wad of newsprint.

May grabbed the front page and looked at the date. It was as she had hoped. They had spent a year with the desert people. But a year had not passed in their own time.

"Evan!" She showed the newspaper to him. "Look at this! Today is the day *after* the picnic at Papago Park!"

He bent over so that the paper almost touched his nose. "I don't believe it!" he said. "That's ridiculous!"

"Ridiculous." May laughed in agreement. "Trust the fluteplayer. He's on our side."

She thought she heard an echoing tinkle of laughter. A single flutelike note. It was probably a mourning dove.

At any rate, her mind was racing ahead to other matters. Their problems were far from over. "We'll have to clean up at a gas station," she murmured.

"I've got to cut off all this hair," Evan agreed.

"I don't know what they'll think." May shook her head. "We've changed so much. And we've only been gone overnight!"

"They'll be too glad to see us to worry about our appearance," Evan said, grinning. "We'll work on a story."

The Apache had pursed her lips and was watching them thoughtfully.

"Into the truck!" Evan cried.

As May swung her legs over the hot metal, she looked out to the side of the dusty road. A few late wildflowers sprinkled the ground. A creosote bush waved its green turpentine-smelling branches. A tall saguaro loomed on the horizon, high above a patch of buckhorn cholla.

It won't be long, May thought, before the prickly pear ripen. And then the saguaro.

She hugged the thought close.

It was always a good time when the saguaro bore fruit.

SHARMAN APT RUSSELL

lives with her husband and two children in a hand-built adobe house in the Mimbres Valley of New Mexico. She grew up in Phoenix, Arizona, where—like May in *The Humpbacked Fluteplayer*—she often visited Papago Park and imagined a wild empty desert of rolling hills and tall saguaros. She began writing stories in the fourth grade, and to this day her favorite books are still about children who suddenly find themselves in another world, one of magic and wonder.

Ms. Russell is also the author of two prizewinning works of nonfiction for adults: a collection of personal essays entitled *Songs of the Fluteplayer: Seasons of Life in the Southwest* and *Kill the Cowboy: A Battle of Mythology in the New West*. Her essays and articles have appeared in many national and literary magazines.

The Humpbacked Fluteplayer is her first book for children.